After Aida

After Aida
by Bunny Shulman

Gray Rabbit Publications
1380 East 17 Street, Suite 2233
Brooklyn, New York 11230
www.FantasticBooks.biz

ISBN 10: 1-5154-2386-7
ISBN 13: 978-1-5154-2386-7

First Edition

*This novel is dedicated to my family
for their continued love,
understanding, and encouragement.*

CHAPTER ONE

The seat next to Irene remained empty.

The house lights dimmed. Crystal chandeliers began their ascent to the high ceiling. The conductor made his entrance, bowed to thunderous applause, and took his position in front of the orchestra. The violinists lifted their bows, the concert bass drummer adjusted the stand, the pianist squared his shoulders, wrists held high over the ivory keys in readiness. The conductor raised his arms, the coat-tails of his tuxedo quivered in response. Anticipation trembled throughout the opera house. The maestro motioned with the slight suggestion of a wave, and the overture's opening strains soared to the highest balcony, a mystical sound of strings. The haunting melody filled the opera house until with a nod of his head, the bass drum rumbled, and the music took on a menacing innuendo.

Irene's formal gown pinched at the waist, and her cold fingers clutched the beaded evening purse. "Don't touch me," echoed and repeated as the last words she'd spoken to him. It hadn't been one of their usual spats; those tireless arguments that went nowhere close to the core. And now, as the curtain rose on the opening scene of *Aida*, so did Irene. A quickstep up the aisle toward the exit, she lifted the hem of her long flowing dress and flew down the two flights, through the vacant lobby, and out into the night air.

Outside on the plaza, a newspaper danced and swirled, twisting and spinning in circles, Irene's pale blond hair coming loose from the combs. There was a chill in the evening air. She stopped in the center of the plaza by the fountain to catch her breath and pull her shawl tight around her shoulders. The season's change brought with it the beginning of fall, leaves first turning a palette of colors until they shriveled on the branch and dropped to the ground below. It was with that first gust of cold air that Irene determined it was the right time. Opening night of the Metropolitan Opera would be closing night on her marriage.

Walking around the plaza, her mind was filled with images of pleasing her husband, doing the expected, subjecting herself to his barrage of words, the worn-out talks that went round and round and got nowhere near her intentions or needs. Her every thought was discounted and subjugated. Oddly, with the decision to end the fifteen years set firmly in her mind, Irene felt no trepidation, only a sense of relief.

As she wandered around the plaza, she thought back to their beginnings, and the ongoing deceit. They had met by mistake. She was young and open to adventure, he was handsome and charming. Oh, how eager she'd been to be the perfect wife, thinking he could fill the ache of her lonely childhood. Little did she know what lay ahead, the blush of first love paling by the second year. She should have called it quits then, on the night of their anniversary.

Clamping down on this memory, Irene again circled the fountain, her thumb playing with the gold wedding band, pushing it up over the knuckle and back again into the grove it had made on her fourth finger. She passed a young couple holding hands and staring into each other's eyes. An older man stood holding onto the handlebars of an ancient bicycle with big fat tires. He nodded to Irene as she moved by him a second time. "Missed the curtain?"

A mere shake of her head was all she could muster. She sat down on the concrete edge of the fountain. The city's sounds traveled across the plaza: the scream of a fire engine, the blaring horns, and the screech of tires pierced the night air. The bright lights at the front of the opera house glittered, and she knew that inside, the elegantly clad audience sat still, listening to the great tenor, his voice clear and strong.

"Shame to miss it. This is one of Verdi's most famous and popular operas."

She turned, and with a quick glance, took in the man. His long-sleeved shirt was neatly folded to the elbow. He swiped at the moisture dotting his forehead with the back of his hand. Grey hair cut close, pleasant square face, crinkly lines across his forehead, the corners of his mouth turned slightly upward, his appearance not at all like the men she served at the soup kitchen each Sunday morning. Adults, their faces gray with cheeks sunken, and children of all ages lined up to be served a hot breakfast. There was an ache in the back of her throat each time she served a hungry child clutching a plate with one hand, an adult with the other, eyes turned down sometimes in shame, other times in fear and hunger.

This stranger moved closer, and looked directly at Irene. "You can get in at the intermission, between Acts I and II."

"No, I'm not going back."

"Really? You'll miss the 'Triumphal March' in Act II. It's the most famous melody. Do you know it?" The man sat down beside Irene, one hand holding his bike the other waving a rhythm as he hummed the opening phrases of the music. "You do know it, don't you?"

A nod of her head. Irene knew the opera began with a secret and ended with Aida and her lover buried alive. She closed her eyes and thought of the wasted tickets and empty seats, typical of her life with the lost days and bare years, the bombardment of his demands, the endless effort to make something of nothing, their marriage a sham. For too long she had lived under her husband's thumb, hanging from a spider web, buried in a loveless marriage.

Irene opened her clutch and took out the ticket stubs. The very least she could do was offer the stubs to this nice man. She pulled her shawl more tightly around herself. "Would you like to catch Act II?"

"Isn't this opening night? Formal night?" He cocked his head to the side, indicating the way he was dressed in khaki pants and sneakers. "They'll surely think I'm a bum." A wide grin took over his face.

"Consider it my good deed for the night. Actually, it's almost time for the intermission."

"And would you…," he raised one eyebrow and his voice took on the quality of a tease, "go in with me?"

Was he was mocking her? There was a twinkle in his hazel eyes that she hadn't noticed before. Pausing, she took a deep breath, held it, and then exhaled with a burst, "What the hell. No one checks tickets after the intermission." She stood. "Lock your bike, and let's go hear about lies and secrets and love and death."

The man, again humming the melody, wound the chain through the spokes. "Yes, Verdi tells it all." He snapped the lock in place, leaned the bike against the concrete surrounding the fountain, then wiped his palms on his tan pants, and, turning to Irene, extended his hand, "Kevin's the name, Kevin Brooks."

"Irene."

He turned, pointed to a luxury apartment building across the avenue. "I live there."

"Oh?" she stammered, caught in her misconception. "I thought…"

"I know what you thought. Shall we?"

She hooked her hand around his elbow. The lobby doors opened for the intermission making advancement to the two seats impassable. After the crush of people passed, they made their way up the grand staircase and down the aisle to the two seats. One was occupied by her husband, Ashford.

CHAPTER TWO

Irene's hands flew to cover her mouth. A step back, she gasped, "You! Why are you here?"

The house lights flickered as Ashford reached for her arm and gripped her wrist with a strong hold, fingers digging into her pale flesh. He tilted his head, thrusting out his chin. Though his words were humble, his voice took on a menacing tone. "I was late, for which I am terribly sorry." There was a threatening sense about his stance. Spite was sugar on his tongue.

She pulled away, swatting at Ashford, and staggered back against Kevin, who stood firm, steadying her balance.

"Don't make one of your scenes, Irene. Sit down. Now!" The words were an order hissed between his tight lips. He again grabbed for her arm, connecting only with her beaded evening purse, which he tore from her grip. "You're making a spectacle of yourself."

Irene tried to move, climb out of the frozen state that took hold of her body. She would drown if she didn't act. Ushers sidled up and down the aisle, settling latecomers to the opening of Act II. Irene reached out for her evening purse, held back from her by a sneering Ashford. The house lights fully dimmed, applause greeted the conductor, who again bowed to the audience's welcome.

Ashford spat a command, "Sit!"

Irene gathered her strength, and lifted the skirt of her long gown. Humiliation raced her up the aisle and mingled with rage and anger. Kevin was close behind. Down the steps of the grand staircase she stumbled, through the vestibule and out into the night air, she crumbled in a heap on the stone plaza. Strangled by the bitter pill of her marriage, she swallowed and bit down on her lip until she tasted the spot of blood.

The pale grey taffeta evening dress pooled around Irene's bent knees; her arms cradled her trembling body. She would like to dig a hole into the pavement and jump in appearing in some foreign place far, far away from Ashford. She held her breath, until there was a roaring in her ears. She could barely hear Kevin's voice.

"I guess he caught you by surprise. Here, let me help you up off the cold stone. You're shivering." He lifted her gently, walked them slowly to the center and settled Irene on the edge of the fountain, where she doubled over on herself.

"Thank you. You're being very gracious." She nodded, wondering if this nice man felt an obligation to her. "You remind me of my uncle."

"Is that meant as a compliment?"

It was after their second anniversary that she'd told her uncle how terribly sad she felt. "Yes. I loved him a lot. I didn't get to see him very often. He didn't want me to marry Ashford, but once I made my bed, so to speak, he said I should lie in it."

Sitting on the cold concrete, Irene shuddered at the slightest glimpse of a memory. And then the shocking memory rolled in like a summer storm. Hands clasped, she squeezed them together, the wedding band digging into her flesh. She had been joyous to share the secret, a secret she had kept from Ashford. In preparation for their anniversary, she had prepared his favorite dinner. With painstaking effort, she had followed the recipe, the aroma drifting throughout their one-bedroom apartment. The table had been set with his grandmother's lace table cloth, their best china and silver along with the elegant champagne glasses from their wedding. The osso bucco simmered on the stove, the meat tender, falling off the bone, while the chilled champagne awaited the pop and fizz. She thought she'd serve this anniversary dinner along with the secret.

At seven she took off her apron, lit the candles, and waited for Ashford. At eight o'clock she paced around the living room, crossed the thick carpet to the wine rack, opened a bottle of red, poured a goblet, pushed it aside, and watched the candles drip onto the cloth. Nine came and went. At ten she dumped the entire dinner in the garbage, and sat stewing in her own fury and disappointment. One glass after another, she filled the goblet, then spilled each glass of the fine burgundy wine down the sink, until the bottle of red wine was empty. She undressed, and got into bed, waking in the morning, her husband was sound asleep by her side, as if nothing was amiss.

She moved from the bed, pulled on underwear and a long t-shirt, crept into the kitchen, and gulped a glass of water. The pounding in her head increased with each swallow, and the odious smell in the open garbage pail brought a flash of last night's dinner. It was then the nausea hit, and a trickle of blood ran along her inner thigh. And when on that awful morning she went back into the bedroom and told Ashford she was having a miscarriage, she was shocked to learn he had never wanted children.

The pain of that moment couldn't be erased. It lived with Irene every moment with every breath. There would never be a family. Her hands ran on the rough concrete lip of the fountain. Gripping the folds of her dress, Irene got up and looked right and left. "Do you have it?"

"Have what?"

"My evening bag. It has to be here."

"What?"

"My purse."

"Your husband grabbed it from you. He must have it."

She stopped for a second, then whipped around and went back toward the opera house saying, "I have to go."

Beads of sweat popped on her forehead and under her armpits, the light grey fabric staining the color to a deep charcoal. At the close of act two, she pushed her way through the crowd, and barged down the aisle to the two empty seats. Bending low, her hands groped under the seats, between them, her cheek brushing against the dirty carpet.

Tugging herself upright, she stumbled over the hem of her gown, the heel of one shoe hitching the hem of her dress until the taffeta ripped. Hair tumbled from the chignon, soft blond tendrils curled around her flushed cheeks, distress ringed her pale blue eyes. "Has anyone seen my purse?"

Irene glanced as the orchestra readied itself for the beginning of Act III, the wedding scene. She knew the lovers would not live on happily ever after, and could only imagine the worst possible scenario for herself. She had good reason.

She stopped an usher, went to the manager, asked the bartender handing glasses of champagne to waiting hands, but no one had seen her husband carrying the lost beaded bag holding the key to her safety deposit box, and the evidence of his fraud, deception, and duplicity.

Irene made her way through the noisy swarm of tuxedos and glittering jewelry to the lobby, and positioned herself under the huge swirling reds and oranges of the Marc Chagall mural. Amidst the buzz of competing voices, her eyes pierced the crowd, searching for Ashford. Up and down the cantilevered stairway, through the main level and down to the lower lounges, she searched to no avail. And when finally the lights flickered, and the lobby emptied, defeated Irene left the building, made her way across the plaza and out to the sidewalk. With the shawl wrapped around her shoulders, she lifted one arm to wave for a taxi, and was hit with the full realization that she had nowhere to go and not a dime to do it with.

CHAPTER THREE

The day had started for Kevin with the discovery that his racing bike had been stolen from the store room of the apartment complex. Dressed and ready to pedal to work on the Porsche bicycle was an everyday event. A birthday present to himself, the cost of $8,000 had been extravagant, but it was 'worth it' to ride a cycle made of chrome and titanium alloy. Every day, he'd don his helmet, swing a leg over the back wheel, go south on Broadway, east on 42nd Street, south on Madison, hand it to the concierge, and be at his office in a timely fashion. His one bid to the environment was to walk or bike whenever possible, avoiding gas powered transportation.

Kevin cursed and kicked the hulking fat tires of the bike left in place of his. The lock and chain lay curled on the concrete floor. He knew only one person would dare to do this: his son. Kevin closed his eyes, and could almost taste the dream of his son in law school, passing the bar and developing into a passionate trial lawyer. But that was not to be. Again, he kicked the ancient bike, hung his helmet on the handle bar, and left the storeroom thinking his son should remain locked behind bars.

Kevin walked to his office, and with each step tracked the growth of his charming son, from infant, to a troubled youth, to a habitual criminal. He'd started small, stealing candy from the corner store, increased as a teen to petty crimes, then onto drugs, progressing to the latest series of drug related events. His son was guilty on all counts but somehow had been released from jail, making his presence known by stealing the precious bike.

Kevin crossed 42nd Street, pulled a tissue from his jacket pocket, and wiped his brow. People brushed past on the crowded sidewalk, cars honked, and taxis swerved to a stop at the corner, barely missing a pedestrian on crutches. Cars and buses on the wide street came to a standstill. A siren screeched off in the distance. Kevin took off his jacket, slung it over his shoulder, stopped, turned back, and instead of going to the office, headed home.

Back in his apartment, he phoned his ex-wife, Gloria. Her husky voice answered on the third ring.

"Whoever this is, should be shot."

"It's only me."

"Who the hell is 'me'?"

"Your first husband."

"Didn't recognize your voice. It's been what…"

"Years." Kevin couldn't help but laugh to himself with relief at no longer placating her vanity. He didn't wait for her to complete thoughts. Her sentences were never total, just like her relationships. Always up for someone to fill in the blanks, or come along with a better offer. "Look, you should know, your son is out of jail."

"It's the middle of the night."

Still dark in California, Kevin imagined her turning in bed, the satin sheets slipping back, her dyed hair in disarray, the sunken cheeks and green eyes naked of make-up; this was not something posted on magazine covers. No, it was the edited digital work the public saw. "It's ten here in New York."

"He's out?"

"Up to his old tricks."

"I need my beauty sleep," Kevin heard her yawning, and then the phone call ended with a click. He cursed the day he'd first seen Gloria. She'd stood in the doorway of the room. Sun light had been sucked out the room and drawn to a beam on her. Up until that moment, it had been a typical Sunday morning with the *Times* crossword puzzle, the only diversion Kevin afforded himself from his studies.

She sauntered over, placed a chin on his shoulder, pulled the fountain pen from his hand, wrote her phone number across the page, and promptly left the room. Like an obedient pet, he had followed, caught up with her, and they married the following month.

Hypnotized by her beauty, he had no one to blame but himself for the wasted two years they had lived together, the birth of a child, and the thirty empty years that followed. On very few occasions did they speak to one another. This was one of those days.

He placed the cell phone on the side table, jumped up from the armchair, called the office, changed his clothes, and then took the old relic of a bike out into the streets to search for his son, the addict. If need be, he'd ride all over the city to find his bike.

It was hard going on the old bike. As opposed to his featherweight of a bicycle, this was an ocean-going liner. With each push on the pedals his resentment grew.

On Ninth Avenue, he stopped at a food truck, leaned the bike against the fender, bought a bottle of water, splashed it over his face, and ate a hot salted pretzel. Back on the bike, knowing this was but a fool's errand, Kevin headed to lower Manhattan and the southern end of Fifth Avenue, Washington Square Park. The old bicycle left under the arch, he walked amongst tourists and watched from the corner of his eye a circle of young men, jabbering and laughing with one another, the sweet smell of pot unmistakable. He wished Nick was one amongst this group of college kids, but his son, after barely graduating high school, had not gotten near college.

"Hey," he sauntered toward the group. "You guys from NYU?"

"Yeah? What's it to you?"

"Just curious. Miss the old days when I came here between classes." He chuckled, and rolled his shirt sleeves up another fold, deciding on a story line. "My kid's here now. Maybe you know him. Nickolas. Goes by Nick. Nick Brooks."

The guy with freckles and red hair asked, "What year, man?"

"Junior."

"I don't know him."

"Don't know him," said another shaking his head.

"Rides a bike everywhere he goes. It's a Porsche bike."

"I'd like to get my hands on a bike like that."

"Maybe you've seen him today?"

"You a cop?"

"Me? No."

It was as if a shark had approached them, the group of students moved away from Kevin like a school of bait fish. He watched them for a few moments, then circled the Mews, checked the chess tables, sauntered the outskirts of the park, and returned to the arch where he mounted the old bike and set forth again, this time for Avenue A, the neighborhood for heroin.

In and out of the narrow streets, he pedaled onward with a sole purpose, barely stopping for a quick hot dog, until finally acknowledging the ineptitude of his efforts. Even if he found Nick and the bike, what then? Their relationship had been ineffectual at best. The few times they were together, the kid was either drunk or stoned, and Kevin couldn't tell the difference. The boy took after his mother with deep green eyes, the color of emerald, dark hair with glints of brushed gold, and an unsatisfied hunger. Kevin had been the guilty provider with an open wallet.

He pushed himself faster, weaving between the cars, bent over the handlebars. Now that the sun had set, happy-hour crowds spilled out to the street. He was but a mere dot pushing himself forward, no longer searching for either the bike or his son. All he sought was to be safe in the familiar areas of uptown with its clean streets, hansom drawn carriages, and Lincoln Center, the hub of culture.

CHAPTER FOUR

The dealer, his hooded eyes vigilant, the baseball cap pulled bill to the back, held the precious bike by the seat. "What do I want with it?"

"Sell it, or, you know, use it," adding with a knowing tip of his head, "It could be a valuable asset in your line of business."

"Hot?"

"No… from my old man."

He moved with accusation closer to Nick. "Worth a thousand to me."

A step back, a mere nod, and the deal was set.

"Where you been, kid?"

"Around."

"Want a touch of heaven? Something to lift you high?"

"No thanks. I'm off the stuff."

A guttural laugh. "As a gift. For old time's sake."

Nick counted the ten C notes, folded the bills, and stuffed them into the pocket of his tight jeans.

"You gonna walk away from this gift of holy heaven?" He jabbed a finger into Nick's muscular chest. "You hurtin' my feelings, man."

"I'm finished. No more of that shit." He touched his fingers to his forehead in a salute, said, "See ya," and walked double-time away from Tompkins Square Park until he flagged a cab, bent his six-foot body, and slid into the taxi. "JFK. Make it quick."

The driver swung onto the FDR Drive, and joined bumper to bumper traffic headed north, the roadway clogged with vehicles of all sizes and shapes driven with impatience, honking and swerving: ineffectual efforts to get ahead of the next car.

"Geez, this is going to take forever."

"Sorry, dis'll ease soon."

Fingertips pressed against the dirty window, Nick squinted in the lowering light, looking out to the East River. "You got the time?"

"Seven."

If Nick could jump from the car and run the rest of the way to the airport, he would. Certainly, if he could push the rest of the cars out of his way, he would. Instead, he sat jittering, the muscles in his legs jerking to move, his body twitching in impatience.

He knocked on the partition. "Hey, get us out of this mess of traffic."

The driver hit his horn in response.

"I don't care what the meter says. Big tip if you get me there before eight."

The driver looked back over his shoulder. "We almost at the bridge."

Nick flung himself back against the seat. "Just get me there."

"Hey Boss, we getting there."

"Just drive."

Across the bridge, onto the side roads, Nick rubbed his hands over his thighs, his thoughts rumbling in disorder. He picked at the cuticle on his right thumb, and bit off the rough edge. As a kid, his mother put Crisco on his hands to keep him from biting his fingernails. He kept on chewing his nails until the tips of his fingers were bloody. Once she made him wear gloves in the summer, but that didn't stop him. The kids made fun of him that year. At the pool, he got back at them, almost drowning the kid they called Fatty, then he stole their wallets from the locker room. He wiped away the memory of his beginnings, and sank lower into the torn seat.

The meter ticked, the tires rolled, horns blared, and finally the cab stopped at the terminal. Nick peeled off the fare and tipped the driver. He raced into the building. If the gods were with him, now was the time he'd start his life all over again. Down the escalator he charged, to the baggage claim area he sprinted, and there, waiting for him, one hand resting on a large black and white checked suitcase, was Riley.

"Hey," he shouted weaving between the luggage. It was but seconds until he reached her, though it seemed to him as though hours had passed. She looked just about the same as before the incident that had torn them apart: a long-ruffled skirt, loose sweater, and wide leather belt slung low over her hips. The ankle boots completed her look. He wondered what he looked like to her as he kissed her gently on the lips.

"Sorry I'm late."

"Well, that hasn't changed." She laughed almost a sigh, and arched back a bit. "And you? How are you now?"

"You'd be real proud. I'm finding my way. It's not easy, but I'm clean."

"Are you?"

"Riley. I could never lie to you."

"Before we go, we must swear to each other, just like we promised, that part is over for us."

He pulled her into a tight embrace and whispered in her ear. "On my life, no more drugs. You are my ecstasy. I promise." He grasped the handle of her roller suitcase in one hand, and led the way out of the terminal into a cab, giving the driver the address of his father's condo.

CHAPTER FIVE

A blister had begun to form on Irene's right foot, the black suede of her low-heeled shoe rubbed against the little toe and heel. Proceeding across Sixty-Sixth toward West End Avenue, she stopped on Amsterdam. Here the street at night was alive. People sauntered at all hours as though there was no need to rush. In her young days, she shared an apartment on the West Side with two other college grads. Discussing world issues as well as matters of the day, they'd stay awake until the wee hours of the morning, then get up early the next day, fresh and alert, and go off to work.

Right out of Hunter College, Irene worked as a secretary for a small law firm. Though a whiz at her job, dictation was not her strong suit. Often, she'd merely get the gist of the information needed, and fill in with her own judgment. Because her writing far surpassed what had been originally intended, she was a favorite of the head partner, a jolly-faced man in his eighties. The day he put his hand on her breast was the day she quit.

At a little all-night drug store, the last of the mom-and-pop pharmacies in the city, Irene pushed open the heavy glass door and entered. She needed a band-aid, a place to rest, a friend. Her eyes scanned the aisles until she spotted the first aid sign. She pulled a box of assorted band-aids off the shelf, slid her fingernail under the closure, took one out, closed the box and put it back on the shelf. She ripped open the paper and bent to place the adhesive on her heel.

A clerk loomed over her stooped body and pointed to the mirror above the aisle. "You gotta pay for the box."

She stood. "Oh." A shock clutched her stomach, waved up her throat, and like a fish caught on a hook she remained, her mouth gaping open.

"Caught you red-handed."

"No. No," she finally muttered and drew in a short breath.

The clerk's starched white jacket, tight around his skinny neck, crackled as he reached to remove the box from the shelf. "Once the seal is broken, I can't sell it."

Her lips tightened. She closed her eyes, shook her head and started for the door.

"Can't let you go, ma'am."

She turned to face him. "I only took one band-aid from the box. No one will notice."

"That's not a nice thing to do, shorting someone else."

"I know, and I'm sorry." She took another step away from the clerk, but he placed a hand on her shoulder, stopping her. His wrist was all sinews and bones, like what she imagined a cadaver's wrist would look like. "Look," she said, a flush had risen from her chest to her temples. "I can come back and pay you. What is it, around five dollars? I'll come back. You can see I don't have my pocketbook or anything on me, and I was getting a blister." She smoothed the wrinkles on her gown. "You can see, I've just come from the theater without my bag." She rolled her empty hands, then tilted her chin with a next thought. "I'll sign an IOU if you want. I'm Irene Aubrey."

He stood unmoved; his dark eyes holes in his gaunt face. His Adam's apple bobbed up and down. "People like you think you're so entitled."

"No, no! That's not it at all." And with another thought, her hands fluttered out to the clerk. "Here, I'll leave my ring with you as a sign of good faith that I'll come back." She pulled the wedding band off her finger and placed it on the counter. "There, that should satisfy you."

With a nod, the clerk looked over the ring, took a pad and pencil, and wrote a receipt, "One gold wedding band inscribed AA loves IA."

CHAPTER SIX

Irene rolled her thumb over the empty indentation on her ring finger, a lasso around her life no longer. She proceeded to West End Avenue, hoping to find a warm hug from Julia. Irene knew she'd be welcome. Best friends in grade school, cheerleaders in high school, and close ever since, she'd find a shelter at her friend's modest apartment.

Irene pressed the buzzer several times before she heard the click of the door lock. An elevator ride to the third floor, the odor of fried onions, and there Julia stood in the hall, bathrobe flung over her nightgown.

"Oh my God, you look a sight." Julia's thin hair hung in limp threads around her pudgy face.

"Sorry I woke you."

"Where are you… oh, never mind." She grabbed Irene in a tight hug. "Come on, Sweetie, tell Momma all about it."

Tears overflowed, her nose dripped, and sobs escaped Irene as she was almost lifted into the apartment. Collapsing on the worn couch, she buried her face in the shawl, her shoulders hunched, and she shook and wept until the sobs became snuffles and she was able to blubber, "A divorce." Little by little the flow of tears stopped, and in their place, she laughed out loud. "Can you believe, after all this time, finally, divorce."

"Are you sure, this time?"

"Definitely."

"You've said this before, but you've always gone back hat in hand."

"Not this time."

"If I know anything at all about Ashford, he'll give you a real hard time. You sure you want to do this?"

"Never so sure of anything in my entire life."

Julia opened a bottle of chardonnay, poured them each a full glass, and curled on the arm chair. "Okay, tell all, and don't leave out any details."

"I'm not sure where to start." She squinted, picturing the changing tide. "We had tickets to the Met, opening night, *Aida*, and were to meet for dinner at Lincoln Square Steak. Naturally, he dressed in the city at the firm's apartment, and I arranged for a car service from home. God forbid he escort me there, but that's something I'm used to happening. Going it alone, I mean. He's so obnoxious to everyone, not just me."

She stopped for a moment, remembering how he had been late, she already seated and looking over the menu. He had barely said a cursory "hello," didn't apologize for being late, and immediately ordered a bottle of fine wine and dinner without looking at either the menu or the wine list. His words were clipped, impatience advancing across his face. He ordered filet mignon, rare, double baked potato, asparagus, al dente and creamed spinach. "And for," he dipped his head and not saying wife, or madam, or the lady, but waved a dismissive hand toward Irene, "salmon and salad."

"Dressing on the side, please," she had added, her soft voice in direct contrast to her husband.

The wine bottle delivered, the pricey red held in reverence by the young waiter, who poured a tiny taste into Ashford's glass. Ashford sniffed the wine, his nostrils widening as his eyes narrowed, and after he took a sip, he almost threw the glass in the waiter's face, but instead poured the liquid on the waiter's white jacket and demanded, "Send the sommelier. He at least has knowledge of food pairing."

Irene looked at Julia. "Honestly, in the quietest voice I could muster, I said he should apologize to the waiter." She took a sip of the chilled white wine. "And you know what his response was? 'Well, if you think he should get an apology, you should go fuck him.'"

Irene took a short breath. "You know, the restaurant was packed with well-heeled before-the-theater-crowd, and I don't know if anyone heard him, but I looked across the table at the man I'd married: an angry, hostile man who was always right. No matter what. I thought I could not go to sleep in the same bed one more night. I know I bowed my head and said as plainly as I could that I wanted a divorce. His hand shot out, and he grabbed my arm and squeezed it in his tight grip. It was like a cuff tightening around my throat instead of my arm. I pulled back, toppling the chair, and fell on the floor. Waiters hustled to help me to my feet. Ashford stood up and again reached for me. I know I screamed out, "Don't touch me. Not ever again."

Irene straightened up, and rubbed at the blister and band-aid. Shaking her head, she held out her empty hands. "And I'm here without a place to go or how to proceed. And to top it all off, everything I have is in the bank vault, and he has the key."

"What? You gave him the key?"

"Are you mad? Of course, I didn't give it to him. I had it hidden in the zipper of my evening bag."

CHAPTER SEVEN

Nick led the way from the elevator, across the marble entry, and ushered Riley into the foyer of the apartment.

The cult of "cool," Riley, her spiky hair dyed Heinz fifty-seven varieties, her face was accentuated by one bushy eyebrow, placed one foot at a time on a straight-backed chair. She unbuckled the ankle boots. "Don't look so worried."

"Maybe I should have told him."

She turned and ran her fingertips along Nick's forehead, drew him close, kissed him on the eyelids, then pressed her lips tight on his mouth. Drawing back, she looked past his shoulder to an overhead chandelier dripping with icicles of crystal. "How long has it been since you've been here? I mean with your dad."

"A couple of years. I told you, he's a tight-ass. Didn't want me around from the beginning."

"You'll see, he'll be happy to have you here."

"I bet," he said, fingering the chain that led from his belt into his pocket. "Maybe we should go to a hotel."

"Don't be silly," she waltzed barefoot into the living room. Her eyes swept the simplistic elegance of the space. "Besides, I like it here."

"It's much better down in the Village. That's where the music is, the clubs, real life, you name it. Shit, there's nothing to do here."

"We'll make our own music."

Nick pulled the checked suitcase down the hall, went into a bedroom, and flicked on the light switch. Riley followed, running her fingertips on the silk wallpaper. "This your bedroom?"

He shook his head, "Nah, I don't really have a bedroom here. Not since I was a kid, even then, I had to stay back in California. That's where she said I belonged." He deepened his voice and stood peering over his shoulder, imitating his mother's stance, "'what Gloria wants, Gloria gets.' Kevin wanted—"

"You always call your father Kevin?"

"Always. He pretty well disowned me when I got, you know, in trouble."

"We're not talking about that incident. Remember, it never happened." She jumped, twisted in the air, and landed flat on her back on the bed, her skirt flying up around her black bikini underwear. Arms opened wide, she said in a dramatic tone, "Come and get it."

CHAPTER EIGHT

Kevin opened the door to his apartment and sensed that something was amiss; a kind of electricity was humming in the air. He placed his keys on the foyer table, his intuition signaling *Nick*. Heaviness overcame his legs, his shoulders slumped as he sat down on the straight back chair in the foyer, arms hung at his sides. He had never really been involved in Nick's life, had avoided too much contact, letting the checks to Gloria assuage his guilt. But here loomed a second chance for both of them.

In the dim light of the overhead chandelier, he noted the pair of women's boots lying askew on the marble floor. With the toe of his sneaker, he nudged them until they were aligned and at attention. Kevin needed order in business as well as balance in his home, where the housekeeper kept paintings centered, chairs around the dining room table aligned, closets organized by color, tabletops void of clutter. He wished his personal life could be so structured and well thought out, for there were those frivolous occasions when a flippant impulse or an unforeseen desire pushed him to act in a spontaneous manner, resulting in regret.

The cell in the back pocket of his khakis chirped the delivery of a message: "Don't neglect Nick. Arriving tomorrow." Included in the brief message was a selfie of Gloria, her green eyes shaded by the half-closed eyelids, the lace see-through dress plunged to her navel, and her bleached blonde hair flowing in a seductive manner. Her face, clear of wrinkles, Kevin could only imagine the surgery and injections used to achieve this appearance of youth. Still beautiful, he was certain heads turned when she entered a room. Deep in his groin he felt the old attraction stir.

He sat quietly in the foyer, conflicted by both excitement and disgust, not wanting to deal with the anticipated problems Nick was certain to bring. The stolen bike was an issue thrust into the back of his mind, but dealing with Gloria and Nick together brought a thickness to his throat. He shuddered at what the days ahead might hold for him.

Checking the cell for further information, he chuckled at the brevity of the message, the incomplete thought of her arrival, and the terse instruction to care for Nick. He stood, and tucked the phone back in his pocket, aware that it was already ten o'clock. Verdi's triumphant opera thumped in his head. *Aida*'s final curtain had probably closed by this time and he wondered what that nice young woman, Irene, thought of the finale, when the unfortunate lovers were buried alive.

In the kitchen he turned on the lights, dimmed the rheostat, pulled a frosty bottle of Heineken from the oversized refrigerator, and poured the foaming beer into a tall glass. He leaned against the granite countertop and took a long drink. The chilled beer slid into his parched mouth and throat while he picked at the dinner of crabmeat left by the housekeeper. From the corner of his eye, he saw a shadow glide past the hall.

Kevin gulped the last of the beer and placed the empty glass in the sink. Mouth clenched tight, he walked into the living room. He expected to see Nick reclining on the couch so he was surprised to see standing by the window a sublime statue. The rays of a full moon shone through the vast windows on to flesh smooth as alabaster, legs sculpted by a ballet master, buttocks small and firm, rounded breasts rising and falling with each breath. The nude figure came to life as the image stirred from its pedestal and moved to the center of the room. The figure held a cigarette and drew a deep inhalation, slowly letting the smoke issue from her open mouth. Kevin stood transfixed, imagining this a reincarnation of Gloria.

Wide-eyed, he watched as the vision strode across the thick carpet, the moon's spotlight following her as though an obedient slave. All he could say was, "We don't smoke in this house."

"I'm Riley."

"Riley?" he blinked.

She snuffed out the cigarette and extended her hand. "And you're Kevin, right?"

A desire to go back to his twenties, or maybe even his thirties, danced in his head. He nodded. "Riley."

She laughed, and bent over the couch. "Nick, wake up. Your dad's home." Standing like a demure child, she placed one hand over her breasts and the other over her dark curly pubic hair. "Sorry, I'm not dressed for the occasion."

CHAPTER NINE

Irene turned from one side to the other on the couch. Her mind, sharp as broken glass, questioned and re-affirmed the decision to file for divorce. Thinking of his fury, she squeezed her eyes closed, her lower lip caught between her teeth. She knew Ashford would be obstinate and unyielding, and the road would be tough. But, rather than crumble, as she had done on prior occasions, she would remain firm. "Not this time," she said under her breath. She pictured his crooked smile, one side of his mouth lifting, before shouting, "Never."

The comfort of sleep illusive, she tossed off the covers and sat on the edge of the sofa-bed, staring into the dark living room. It resembled the apartment in which she and Ashford had lived the first two years of their marriage. To Irene, it had the charm of a cottage, decorated with garage-sale odds and ends, chintz upholstery, and flowered curtains. Ashford said it was undignified and beneath his class. He made it abundantly clear one morning. She could still hear his voice thunder and bounce off the walls.

"Get with it, damn you. I can't have my clients here. It's a dump." He threw the morning newspaper across the table, pages flying to the floor. "A man in my position needs a proper place. I'm buying a big house."

"We can barely afford this apartment."

Ashford smacked his hands flat on the table "Take that look off your face. I know what's best."

She had stood meekly aside at the purchase of the large house on Long Island, with a shockingly large mortgage. Her voice buried, the pen shook between her fingers when the contract was slid across the table for her signature.

Irene turned onto her back, and staring up at a small crack that tiptoed across the ceiling, wondering if Julia intended to repair it. She remembered when Ashford and his mother hired a painter to design a mural for the dining room, and when it was done, it depicted an ancient time, a cracked stone wall from some Greek mythology. Ashford said it created a sense of immortality. Irene thought it depressing.

Under the blanket Irene lay still, fuming at her younger self, the submissive twenty-three-year-old being. She'd been looking at a furniture catalog, every page crammed full of possible furnishings for their cavernous house, when her mother-in-law took the book from her hands, and tossed it aside, saying, "None of that will do."

Irene's body jerked. "What's wrong?"

"That stuff is cheap looking. Ridiculous."

"There's a velvet couch I like and a—"

"No! We're not shopping at the bottom of the heap." She pulled open a leather bag, took out a glossy magazine, and pointed her manicured finger to a picture of a decorated living room. "Now, just look at that!" Tapping her fingernail on the page, her diamond flashing, she said, "This is elegance."

Irene could feel the sharp eyes of her mother-in-law glaring at her as she peered at the photograph of an impersonal showroom with high backed chairs in flocked fabrics, settees upholstered in silk brocade, and lamps dripping with crystal. "It's very, ah, stiff. I can't imagine who lives in a formal living room like this."

"Ashford and I love this look."

"Really?"

"Down to the very last accessory."

"It's not very inviting."

"Ashford has bought it all, with my guidance, of course."

Overpowered by both her husband and domineering mother-in-law, Irene sank lower into the role of window-dressing. Small and inadequate, she did as she was told and entertained Ashford's business associates, conducting herself appropriately when the occasion called for her attendance, melting into the backdrop of draperies and carved woodwork.

Gone were his thoughts of starting a foundation to help those less fortunate, a trait that had drawn her to him early in their dating phase. No longer did he talk of enriching young lives. And before too many years had passed, Irene knew it was only time before he sought a younger version. She'd stayed the quiet mouse of a wife until that turning moment when she overheard Ashford on the phone yelling at his secretary. "Fix it, or I'll fix you."

Later that night, she asked, "What was that phone call about?"

"Nothing to do with you." He took a fist-full of pistachio nuts from the crystal bowl, dropping the opened shells carelessly, and popped the nuts into his open mouth.

"What made you so angry? You were about to explode."

His cold eyes bore into her. "None of your business."

"I'm just curious, that's all."

"Get this straight: my business is my business."

It was simply out of curiosity that she'd asked him, but he'd turned like stone and removed himself from the house, slamming the front door. The following week, Irene opened a safe deposit box in her own name, and from that day on, she squirreled away a small percentage of the household money. It had all started with simple curiosity.

Kicking off the blanket, she groped her way into the small kitchen, made a cup of instant coffee, foraged in the refrigerator for something to eat, and sat at the counter nibbling on a cheese stick until the morning light seeped around the edges of the shaded windows.

Julia tapped her on the shoulder. "Morning." She bent over the half-filled cup of coffee and wrinkled her nose. "Ugh, you need real stuff this morning." She chose an intense flavored capsule, and dropped it into the shiny espresso machine. "This'll clear the cobwebs. It's the best. Did you sleep?"

"Not a bit. I couldn't stop from conjuring up all sorts of dead ends. I know Ashford'll stop at nothing, not cause he loves me or anything like that; it's his ego. I'm his possession, something he can buy or sell, but never give up. He can't stand a loss of any kind, much less the loss of his wife and the publicity it will bring. If he can, he'll cut me off and wait for me to come crawling back."

"Ha. He's in for a surprise. Have you told him point blank that you are going to file?"

"No. Don't you think I should get a lawyer first, and just have the papers delivered to Ashford?"

"Are you afraid to face him?" Julia placed a dainty cup of double espresso on the counter in front of Irene, the aroma curling like velvet, smooth and strong.

"No, I'm not afraid of him. I don't think he'd ever be physically violent to me."

"Verbal abuse is just as harmful. Irene, face it, you're the very definition of an abused wife. If I were in your shoes—and of course, I'm not and thank God never have been—I'd have left the bastard years ago."

Irene smoothed her fingertips over the edge of the espresso cup. "But, you know me: if I can avoid a confrontation, I will. It's almost like I'm afraid of taking a misstep. I don't want to go back to what I was before I met Ashford. I want to begin a new life."

"You were pretty cute, you know. A little sassy."

"We did have fun in those days."

"Like waiting tables at fund-raising events."

Irene pursed her lips. "The galas were elegant affairs, every one of them. Actually, I forgot you got me that job with the catering company."

"Yeah. And that's how you met Ashford, the dashing up-and-coming lawyer."

"We were on staff at the event raising money for the homeless."

"Everyone who mattered in the city was there."

"Ashford's mother organized the event and had spilled champagne down the front of her gown. I'd tried to help dry the front of her designer dress, but Ashford said he'd take care of it himself. I watched him usher his mother through the crowd and seat her at the head table. And then when he turned back and introduced himself to me, he oozed self-confidence and charm."

"He hypnotized you with his gift of sweet talk. That man molded you as if you were clay."

"God, he was easy with the words. Blunt but alluring, I thought he'd take care of me. He was going to be my protector. I was painfully naïve"

"Protector, be damned. He suffocated you."

"What I thought was his confidence, was his need to control. If I give him the chance, he'll whip me back to that well-trained wife. If I give him the opportunity…" Her eyes focused on the ceiling. "It's like I've had brain surgery, and now I'm ready to start rehabilitation."

"Just put one foot in front of the other. You'll do great. Look, you can stay here as long as you need to. But if I were you, I'd rent an apartment immediately, go home and pack my belongings, and anything else I might want. My best advice is for you to make as clean a sweep as you can."

The double espresso had stirred her pulse. "I do have a plan."

"You always had a plan."

"There's an attorney I'll call later today."

"I assume you have enough money tucked away."

"Enough for a while." She looked at the clock hanging on the wall over the stove. "I have to get to my bank first thing this morning to make sure Ashford doesn't gain access to my vault."

"Even if he found the key in your evening bag, he won't know what it's for, will he?"

"He'll know."

"Will he try to…"

"You never know what he's capable of. He's a skilled manipulator. Charming when he wants, and a snake at the same time." Irene slipped down from the bar stool. "I'll take the train out this morning. Get there before he has a chance."

Julia put a hand out. "Stop. Banks are closed today. It's Sunday."

CHAPTER TEN

A nightmare disturbed Kevin's sleep, but once he was awake, he couldn't remember any of it. But a foul mood had been set, and followed him into the shower, stared back from the mirror at his face while shaving. The bad temper circled him while dressing for Sunday until with a start, he remembered Nick and his nymph were there in the apartment, and Gloria would be arriving sometime during the day.

What he foresaw were hours of recriminations, with Gloria strutting around the apartment appraising each accessory, Nick swearing on all that was holy that this time he meant to be clean, and Riley taking it all in with her doe eyes.

He'd been looking forward to today's physical challenge on the tennis court, his backhand strong, forehand swift on the attack, but his serve needed help. What he needed was focus and control. A scowl crossed his face. He texted his tennis partner and cancelled their singles match and lunch date.

He strode from his bedroom and down the hall. His senses acute, he heard not a sound coming from the guest bedroom. Though he questioned Nick's choice of girlfriend, he was somehow proud for his son to have latched on to someone of such unabashed loveliness and uninhibited self-awareness.

He buried himself in the newspaper, his foot jiggling up and down, and completed the *Times* crossword puzzle with his fountain pen. He stood, and paced back and forth in the living room, then went into his study and closed the door. He flipped open the laptop, checked his calendar for the coming week, then swivelled in his chair to the view from his window.

High over the rooftops where he always strove to be: top of his class, chairman of the board, king among men, hero to the multitudes. He laughed to himself, thinking he'd done well enough. He should be content, not question himself. He sat, elbows on his desk, rubbing his temples. When is enough ever enough?

His fingertips trailed on the almost invisible scar over his right eye, the result of a gang of kids pushing him off his very first two-wheel bike, causing him to fall on a gravel path. He'd gotten right back on the bike, not stopped by blood gushing from the open wound, and running into his eye. He hadn't been stopped by fear of the bigger boys, but fought back. He wasn't one to be bullied, not then, and not now.

Turning back to his desk, he glanced at the clock, and saw it was still quite early. He had plenty of time for a jog. He hadn't run in weeks, and his muscles told him so. He changed into a track suit, left a note for Nick on the kitchen counter, and set off for a run through Central Park. Closed to traffic on Sunday, he entered at Eighty-Sixth Street.

A choice of paths, he opted for the loop around the Reservoir on the soft cinder pathway. It was flat, just a little slope on the far side of the mile and a half route. Running a slow pace, he was nonetheless winded when he reached the north side, but proceeded toward the Meadow, where mallards and geese fluffed their wings to the audience of runners. At last he circled back, fatigued and gasping. He leaned on a huge boulder, then sat, resting before returning to what he anticipated to be a long and arduous day.

He watched two teens whisper to one another as they walked by, arms slung around each other's shoulders. A homeless man dragged his overflowing wagon across the grass, and lay down on a park bench. A group of race-walkers, looking like a flock of ostriches, zipped past, their arms pumping low, hips swiveling in exaggeration of the cadence.

A smile crossed Kevin's face, the foul mood of earlier this Sunday dissipated. Coming toward him, he watched a young man swoop a red-headed boy high to sit atop his shoulders. Freckles adorned the boy's face, his cheeks rosy pink. The child threw his arms high in triumph. "Daddy! I'm king of the mountain."

Giving the youngster a thumb's up, Kevin said, "Yes, indeed you are." He watched father and son glide past. His eyes followed the bright orange plaid shirt, thinking that he'd never lifted his son to be king, his attempts at fatherhood continually thwarted by Gloria at every turn. And he'd let her. He pursed his lips. Perhaps it was not too late for him to be a good father to Nick.

CHAPTER ELEVEN

Irene borrowed pants, a plaid shirt, and a fuzzy lavender sweater from Julia's closet, and slipped her bare feet into a pair of loafers, everything at least two sizes too large for her small figure. Arms linked, Julia and Irene strolled at a leisurely pace, crossed the wide avenue, stopped to share a cinnamon roll, and continued to Central Park.

Though the sky was overcast, the Park drew people to its heart, especially on an early fall day when the trees were bedecked in their finest gowns, the hills a canvas of autumn color.

Julia stopped and pointed. "Just look at that view. Doesn't that just make you a believer in all that is good?"

"You're sounding very much like a romantic."

They passed a ballfield where a group of young men were just taking the field. Bike riders, some young on tricycles, rode rented bikes as though they owned the path. Runners in shorts and skimpy tops, sweat pants and sneakers, raced by. Irene and Julia continued on until they heard the magical carousel and caught the smell of hot dogs and popcorn.

Julia bent to tie a loose shoe lace. "I come here every Sunday."

"Whenever we were in the city, my uncle would take me to the Central Park Zoo. That was a special time. Oh, and cotton candy. That sweet, delicious cloud of sugar used to get stuck in my hair." She laughed and wrinkled her nose.

They stood on the fringes and listened to the music. After a moment, Julia waved both arms in time with the music. "I love the calliope, all that wind pushing through the whistles."

"Hey, I've been so involved with myself, I haven't asked you how the rehearsals are going."

"It's great. We're a full orchestra. There are so many talented people in this city. When we all get together, it's almost a party atmosphere, but with strictly serious undertones. I'm so happy there. You know music is my life. I can only bear to teach a few hours a week, so the orchestra is my reward."

"Remember how we started out in grade school, you on a clarinet, when all you wanted was a flute, threw a real temper tantrum until you got what you wanted, and I wouldn't let anyone else near the piano." Chuckling, she said, "All the other kids got the violin. We sure were stubborn."

"If someday I run into that awful teacher, I'll tell him what I really think. God, he didn't know anything about music, and nothing about kids. Always yelling. Amazing we both stayed with our music at all."

"Ashford only bought a baby grand to impress his clients, but I loved it. If he'd known how much I cherished it, he'd probably have sold it just to spite me. He hated it when I played. Sometimes when I feel the ivories under my fingers, the touch is hard to explain. It's silk and satin and sculpted stone at the same time. When I get an apartment, I can rent a piano, even if there's only room in the bathroom for an upright."

Irene fussed with the ill-fitting jeans, raised her gaze to a flock of birds settling in the maple trees, thinking she'd like to join them on their flight south. Her attention was caught by a young man strolling along the path towards them. He was wearing a bright orange plaid shirt and was holding hands with a freckle-faced young boy with eyes big and dark as shiny black marbles.

"Morning," Irene said as the pair drew close.

"Gorgeous day, wouldn't you say? 'Tis a day for the youngun." He swung the boy up into the air, and caught him and whirled around.

The boy screamed with laughter. "Again, Daddy. Again."

The laughter should have been infectious, lightened Irene's heart, lifted her spirits. Instead, tears moistened her eyes. She watched them until they were lost in a crowd of race-walkers. She ducked her head, unbuttoning and then fumbling, buttoned the top buttons of the sweater. "I have to go home, at least to get some clothes, and search for that key. Get stuff for a few days and…. Please, will you come with me? I don't want to be there by myself. We can catch the noon train out, and come right back in. And I'll treat you to dinner at Louis's."

"As if that would tempt me."

"Please do this for me."

She grabbed Julia's arm and pulled her along the path back toward Central Park West. "If we hurry, we can make the express train out of Penn Station."

Julia rolled her eyes. "Oh, this is not going to be pretty."

CHAPTER TWELVE

Heading for home, Kevin stopped and purchased a spiral honey-baked ham, sausages, a two-pound hunk of Vermont cheddar cheese, and a mushroom quiche, all the makings of a sumptuous breakfast, envisioning a fresh start with his son. Once in the apartment, he dropped the shopping bags in the kitchen and went down the hall. He stopped mid-step at the open doorway of his office. Nick was sitting behind the desk with the lap top open in front of him.

"You really ought to clean this mother out."

"What are you doing?"

"Just getting rid of the clutter."

"You don't know what—"

"Old websites. Old software. Wading through this—"

"Stop whatever you're doing."

Startled, Nick pushed back and thrust both hands up. "Whoa."

"Just stop."

"Go figure, I try to do something helpful, and you blast me for it."

"What makes you think you can just come in here and open my computer?"

"What's your problem?"

"It's personal."

"Think I'm goin' to check your bank account, find where you have your money? I don't want anything from you." He closed the laptop and pushed it across the desk, jumped up from the chair and stormed from the room.

Not waiting for the elevator, he took the stairs, flew down the seven flights, and went out of the building, his pulse beating along with a growing temptation, the addiction with its ever-present carrot dangling in front of each step he took. He paced in front of the building. He crossed the street. He went to the corner. Zig-zagging back and forth, he stomped and fumed. He looked up at the apartment, yelled out loud, "Fuck you!" pulled a leftover joint from his back pocket, lit up and strode west, leaving Riley to fend for herself.

Nick thought of himself as handsome. His jeans were fashionably tight, and the jacket he wore had numerous pockets and zippers, the boots were scuffed and in need of a shine. He treaded along Amsterdam Avenue, passed tourists gawking at the high buildings in the midst of being erected, the cranes awaiting action, shoppers rushing, a trio of soldiers at leisure.

His eyes dilated, he squinted in the sun, then peered into a drug store, the temptation of a high within reach. Drugs were just a few feet away. He walked in, strolled the empty aisles, and heard the ka-ching of the old cash register. The lone customer took her bag and waddled out of the store. Nick circled the small store and moved to the front, inhaling the antiseptic smell, his focus on the back pharmacy.

Near the front counter, he knocked over a display of sunglasses. Nick set the exhibit upright, selected a pair of aviator glasses and put them on, adjusting them on the bridge of his nose, his eyes hidden behind the dark lenses. He peered into the small mirror, turning his face this way and that, the price tag hanging over his nose. Leaning across the counter, he asked the clerk, "What do ya think?"

"They're okay, I guess." The clerk shrugged, his high forehead a map of wrinkles.

"Slow day?"

"Sundays are slow."

Nick's eyes shifted to the overhead mirror reflecting the narrow aisles. He leaned further across the counter, one hand in a pocket of the jacket, imitating a firearm. His chin thrust forward, the tone of his voice menacing, he hissed, "What do you think now?"

Fidgeting with the buttons on his shirt, the clerk said, "They're okay."

Slipping the dark glasses down to the tip of his nose, Nick, with eyes of steel, looked over the top of the glasses. "Ever been held up?"

The clerk backed up, mouth gaping open.

Nick laughed, took his hand out of the pocket and stood. With all the nonchalance of the entitled, he dropped the glasses on the counter. "Only kiddin' with you."

He strode out of the drugstore and headed back toward his father's apartment, his chest puffed like a stalking rooster. He carried a sense of arrogance, took command of the sidewalk, marching a straight path back to Kevin's apartment and the hidden stash.

CHAPTER THIRTEEN

Kevin turned on the oven, tore the paper off the still-warm quiche, the comforting aroma of warm, melting cheese filling the kitchen. He bent to place it in the oven, and was startled by Riley walking barefoot into the kitchen. He turned and the quiche, teetering on his fingertips, fell to the floor. "Shit."

"Here, let me." Riley bent to retrieve the aluminum dish, the t-shirt she wore riding high on her shapely thighs. She placed the quiche on the counter, adjusted the oven knob, and turned her chocolate eyes on Kevin. "There. Is that breakfast or lunch?"

"Either. Or both. Whatever you want."

She stretched and yawned, "Where's Nick?"

"He went out." His glance shifted around the room. He did not want to focus on this stunning young woman. "We had a problem."

"Little or big?"

Kevin raised his shoulders. "I don't know. We're not close."

"Well, that's an understatement. You barely know each other."

Kevin turned to the espresso machine. "Coffee?"

"Sure." She opened the refrigerator and stopped. "May I?"

"Cream and pull out the sausages and," he pointed his finger, "the eggs."

Riley placed everything on the counter. "There! I can make a pretty good breakfast, if it's okay with you."

"Be my guest."

Kevin stepped aside, watching her feline body move under the thin fabric. He wondered how it would feel to have a youngster like this curl herself around him. She was without a doubt the picture of youth. He thought of an adult version: Gloria. Both were beautiful women.

He watched as Riley drew utensils from drawers, bowls from the cabinet, bending and lifting. Each movement slow and smooth, like that of a lyric dance, her torso curving and reaching. She tapped one egg after another onto the side of the bowl and let it drip through her fingers. Her fingernails were short and polished a dark purple, a silver ring was on each thumb.

Hardly able to rip his eyes from her, he heard music, the sensual building of erotic tension in Ravel's *Bolero*. He shifted his focus and steadied himself, placing a palm on the granite counter top. "Breakfast starts me off with energy."

"Nick and I were responsible for breakfast out at the place."

"What place was that?"

"The rehab, where we met."

"I wondered where you two met."

"He'd been in for a while before I got there. It was his second time, and I was a newbie." She raised her one bushy eyebrow, and gave Kevin a big smile. "We just gravitated to each other. We're each other's support system. You know...no, I guess you don't know." She busied herself slicing the sausage links and placing them in a fry pan, then turned toward Kevin. "Have you ever been on drugs?"

His gaze narrowed. "That's getting pretty personal, don't you think?"

"I'm only asking cause, you know, it could be genetic. You know, hereditary. They say addiction doesn't just come out of nowhere and besides, he's had a rough life."

"Really! He's had it rough? He doesn't know what rough is. He never wanted for anything."

Riley took a step forward, her hands on her waist, the t-shirt taut against her body, the hardened nipples pointed straight at Kevin. "You think he had what he needed?"

"I don't know what he thinks having it tough is. His mother, she gave him everything."

"Yeah, everything but you, his father."

Kevin swallowed and clenched his jaw. So shaken by the truth, the buzzing of the intercom went unheeded. It took a moment for Kevin to regain his composure and answer the doorman announcing the arrival of Gloria.

Relieved the conversation with Riley had ended, he was hopeful this visit with Gloria would be short and not filled with regrets. They had parted as friends, without the usual recriminations that absorbed so many divorces. He stood in the open doorway of his apartment, listening to the whirring sound of the elevator. His fingertips worried the scar above his eyebrow, and when the elevator door finally slid open, Gloria stood surrounded by suitcases, a red beret tilted to the side, her hair bleached so blonde, it appeared white.

A smile broke across her face, and her throaty voice rang out and bounced off the marble floor of the entry foyer. Deep in his memory, despite himself, he felt her magnetism; the feeling of holding her tight against his chest. When they were together, time had no meaning.

"Kevin, you're gawking."

With a few long strides, she was at his side, hugging his rigid torso and pecking him on both cheeks. Her hands grasped his waist, and she jiggled him. "Don't just stand there."

There was a thickness in his throat. "Gloria."

"Aren't you glad to see me?"

"You look good, really wonderful."

"I've come back."

"You're moving back to New York?"

"With you."

The creases on his forehead deepened, unmoored by her simple statement. Words stumbled as though he'd lost his voice. "What? You hate the city."

"That was long ago."

"What the devil are you talking about? Would you please finish one single thought, and not keep this a guessing game."

"Kevin, don't be like that. Spoil everything." Her fingertips skimmed over his unshaven face.

"What are you thinking?"

"I'm moving back in with you." She called out over his shoulder, "Nick. I'm home."

"Gloria. You're living in a dream world. You can't just move in here." Even as he said this, he thought of their early days together; the gaiety of their youthful exuberance, all the frills of the unknown, their innocence. Kevin looked at the angles of her face, the image caught on magazine covers, the emerald eyes sparkling, the lipstick perfectly applied, famous for her winning smile. Never satisfied, she kept on changing agencies, places, husbands, searching for a something better, and now had come full circle back to the beginnings.

Gloria moved through the foyer and quickly into the living room, her spike heels clicking on the marble. "Nick. It's Mom. I'm home."

"He's not here."

"Where is he?"

Kevin shook his head. "I don't know. We had a squabble and he stormed out of here a while ago."

Riley, still barefoot but dressed in jeans and a short tank revealing her midriff, came walking into the room, her hand extended. "Hi, you must be Gloria."

Kevin was struck by their similarities as Riley, a younger version of Gloria shook hands. It was the posture, that smile, the sexual allure leaking from every pore, the hard edges smudged by the disparity of their ages. They stood facing each other.

"This is Nick's friend, Riley."

Gloria's eyes took in Riley from head to toe—the tight jeans, the ring in her navel, the spiked hair—and shook her hand. "And do you know where my son is?"

"He'll be back soon." Riley glanced at Kevin and back to Gloria. "Wow, Nick has your green eyes. Lucky guy."

No one moved until Kevin found his equilibrium. He tightened his jaw to not be pulled along by Gloria's will. "I'll just move your luggage from the elevator into the entry foyer."

CHAPTER FOURTEEN

A subway ride, a sprint through Penn Station, Irene and Julia raced down the concrete stairs to track twelve, and with barely a moment to spare, boarded the train to Manhasset. The doors closing behind them, they flopped onto seats.

Julia rested the side of her head against the window. "Whew. I'd forgotten you were on the track team."

"I almost lost one of your shoes on the steps."

"So, then you'd be a Cinderella—"

She placed the back of her hand on her forehead in mock despair. "Oh woe is me, I'd be the cinder child."

"Nope, you're no damsel in distress." She laughed. Her lips turned upward, and then as she looked at Irene—whose eyes were closed tight— her laugh stopped. She tilted her head. "You okay?"

"Just trying to get a handle on myself."

"Seems to me you're holding up fairly well."

Irene blinked, gathering her thoughts, her thumb rubbing the indentation on her left finger. "Maybe on the outside, but honestly, I'm terrified."

Julia took hold of Irene's hand. "You'll be fine, whatever you decide to do."

She pulled her hand away. "What do you mean? I told you, I've definitely decided. It's just, you know, he's going to be tough to go against."

The train pulled out of the dark tunnel, picked up speed, and continued on. Irene listened to the clacking of the wheels, and glanced out the window at the passing houses. Some back yards were tended with care— here and there a jungle gym, a wading pool, a child's red wagon tipped on its side, all evidence of family life—while other yards were overgrown, unkempt, strewn with an open refrigerator or an abandoned car.

Across the aisle, a young child sat curled in a woman's lap, whimpering just loud enough to be heard over the sound of the metal wheels rapping on the tracks. The conductor approached and stood, his feet planted wide, and waited while Julia fished in her wallet for a credit card.

"Manhasset. Two, round trip, please."

Irene closed her eyes for what she thought but a moment, but to her surprise, when she glanced again, off in the distance, she saw light bouncing off the gentle waves of Manhasset Bay. The train slowed, and Irene knew they were on the one track trestle, almost there to a house that had never been a home.

The train screeched around a curve. Irene leaned against Julia. "You get married for better or for worse, and you really don't know what to expect of each other. Truth is, I just hope I have enough strength to face this without too much of an ugly fight. That's probably naïve of me."

"You were never naïve."

She leaned in real close and whispered to Julia. "This time I'm prepared. Ashford has always underestimated me. He kept so many secrets, often away on business, phone calls late at night. I was certain of his infidelities. I'm not proud of it, but I foraged through his home office, pried open the locked desk drawers, and found piles of neatly organized papers. They were all held under lock and key. Some dealt with our personal finances, but there were others that were off-putting: tax returns, trust agreements, wills, financial statements, mortgages. I made copies of everything."

It was a short taxi ride to the circular driveway of the Aubrey house, a large two-story white colonial set high atop the three acres of rolling manicured grass and trimmed evergreen bushes. Window shutters were painted glossy black. Irene had suggested Delft blue, but had been outvoted by Ashford's mother. On either side of the double entry doors stood ceramic pots overflowing with yellow mums and dripping with ivy.

Irene reached behind a shutter to get the hidden house key, while Julia paid the driver. They entered the house, and once in the vestibule, Julia took off her shoes, whispering, "Is he here?"

"Don't think so. He's probably with his mother. Sunday brunch at the Club. A Sunday ritual. Their private time."

"Are you kidding?"

"That woman has him under her thumb. I don't really care anymore. Haven't for a long time."

Up the curved staircase and down the wide hall, Julia trailed behind Irene into the master bedroom, where an enormous bed took center stage as an island on the soft grey and cream striped rug. The room was forgiving, a replica of Irene's soothing personality, and the joke was, it was the only place in the entire house that was "hers." She'd fought to decorate this room, and she'd won this battle during their first year in the house. It was a calm place, a refuge for Irene, but not when Ashford was home. Then it became a tense, unyielding place where icicles grew.

Irene opened the door to her enormous walk-in closet, all fitted with drawers and shelves and hanging spaces. She looked over her shoulder and said, "I could sleep in here and he'd never know the difference."

Quickly, she changed out of Julia's ill-fitting clothing, putting on jeans, a pullover, and a pair of loafers. She packed one large suitcase, mindful of the limited space at Julia's apartment. Her hands smoothed over the fabric of a plaid jacket, and she pushed it aside. She shook a leather coat, fingered a cashmere cape, then put her hand in the pocket of a mink floor length coat and pulled out one-hundred dollar bills. Folding the bills, she stuffed them in her pocket.

Julia's eyes widened. "That'll be the day when I find money stuffed away."

"It's my 'madmoney'."

She pulled open the top drawer of the built-in dresser, fumbling around in search of her wallet, groped in her everyday Gucci bag, and to her relief, found her wallet with all her identification.

The sound of a car on the gravel driveway brought Irene from the closet to the bank of windows. Color drained from her face. Her body stiffened, and her voice was lower than a whisper. She talked through a clenched jaw. "I have a grotesque memory-picture of my father prancing around the house with his schlong hanging down. His stream of women flashes before me. I swore I'd never stand for the treatment my poor mother suffered. And here I am, rooted in ugly memories."

Julia put her arm around Irene's waist. "You'll do just fine. You're strong, stronger than you think."

Irene shook her head as though in disbelief. "I can't believe the verbal abuse both my mother and I took. My father made her life miserable. He was a cruel man. He broke her. I know she died of a broken heart." She pressed the back of her hand against the tears that welled in her eyes. "All my childhood, I ached for my mother's love. But he had emptied her out, used her up, and she had nothing left to give or feel. I was angry for her, and lonely for myself."

Irene placed her palms flat on the window pane, and pressed her forehead against the cool glass. "I can't believe how stupid I've been. I married my father."

CHAPTER FIFTEEN

At the slam of the front door, Julia called a cab and Irene, steadying herself, pulled the suitcase off the bed and onto its wheels. "This is it."

Irene, tugging the suitcase, one step placed after another as though nearing a landmine, went into the hall. Julia slung a leather tote over her shoulder and followed closely behind.

When Ashford reached the top of the curved staircase, he stood on the last step, glaring into Irene's flushed face. His eyes lowered to the suitcase and seemed to flicker. "Vacation, my dear?"

Irene steeled herself but did not answer.

"Cat got your tongue?"

Julia put her hand on Irene's shoulder, and whispered in her ear, "Tell him."

"You need a break from all this luxury? Is that it?" He took the last step up and moved closer.

Her throat closed, swollen around words. Her body trembled like the last leaf on the old maple tree. A little shake of her head was her only reply.

"If you walk out of this house now, don't you ever even think of returning."

Irene took a step back, bumping against Julia, who remained firm as a stone wall. "Tell him."

"If you think for one moment of divorce, you'd best shake that little thought right out of your dumb head. You're a failure. Face a few facts. Nothing you have ever done is worthy of me and my heritage. You're one dumb piece of ass, and that's all. Don't you ever forget what I've done for you."

The words were like dulled knives sawing at her. How could she have lived with this wicked man for fifteen years? She would not bleed over him, not give him the satisfaction, not allow herself to be mistreated one more second of her life. "Divorce, Ashford."

"Don't you dare."

He was so close she smelled his breath reeking of kippers and cigar smoke. She tightened her grip on the handle of the suitcase. "I'm leaving now."

He laughed. "You're counting on alimony. I can tell just by looking at your dull face. Think you're going to get money out of this? Think again. You won't have a pot to piss in." He took a step closer. His nostrils flared. "You won't get a penny."

With all her strength mustered, Irene picked up the suitcase, and shoved it against Ashford's chest. He staggered back just enough for her to squeeze past him, and rush down the staircase and out of the house.

Ashford yelled after her, "You ungrateful bitch! I'll sue you for desertion. That'll teach you something about the real world."

Irene couldn't contain the mix of laughing and crying at the same time. "I did it!"

"Oh my God, you certainly did."

"I've never felt so alive in my life."

"I'm so proud of you."

Irene tilted her face toward Julia. "I don't know that I could have done it without you here."

Julia looked with anxious eyes down the empty driveway. "Where the hell is the cab?"

Ashford yelled from the window. "You'll be homeless. That's what you deserve," and slammed down the window.

The cab turned into the driveway, and Julia grabbed the handle of the suitcase. "I thought for a moment you were going to push him down the stairs."

"The thought did occur to me."

"He's a real bastard. None of those things he said about you are true."

"I hope not."

The driver jumped from his cab and shoved the luggage into the trunk. Julia slid in followed by Irene, who climbed in on shaky legs while Ashford's voice followed her, shouting, "You're worthless. I'll make your life a misery."

Irene turned her palms up and looked at her empty hands. "And you really don't mind my staying with you until I find a place?"

"Stay as long as you want. It'll be fine, a little crowded and," she grinned, "you'll be cramping my style, but okay, of course it will be fine."

Ashford opened the front door shouting, "You spineless piece of shit."

CHAPTER SIXTEEN

While Kevin showered, shaved and dressed, he couldn't shake recurring thoughts of Gloria; even more beautiful while pregnant, nude photographs of her swelling body had appeared on the cover of magazines. As the day drew near, much to his dismay, she'd arranged for the birth to be witnessed and filmed, and the baby's first breath recorded.

Kevin wanted this private moment shared with no one. Instead, millions were privy to the images, and Gloria became one of the most photographed models in the history of the indulged glory girls of high-end fashion. Keen to stay on top of fashion, her wardrobe was extensive and —Kevin knew better than anyone—expensive. Her tastes ran to extremes, her thoughts ragged, her intentions never clear. Though Gloria remained dear to his heart, she was hurtful and self-indulgent. He vowed he would not allow her back into his life. Though she was his long-lost love, she was also a mystery.

Holding a cold washcloth to his forehead, Kevin's thoughts were sprinkled with Nick. He dried his face thinking his son was like a distant relative you see once very few years and have nothing to say to, nothing to share with, no path to understanding. He was a puzzle holding the same emerald eyes, a piercing look of inquiry. More times than not, the eyes delved deep into a façade's underbelly, shearing off pretense.

His palms flat on the marble counter, he swore to hold his temper, and resist accusing his son of past sins, and lies, and thefts, even of the stolen bike. Perhaps, Kevin thought, this might be their last chance. Looking in the mirror above the sink, Kevin acknowledged that he was good at straight lines, circles and curves, weights and measures. He'd find a way to get through to Nick.

Down the hallway to the open door of the guest bedroom, Kevin peered in. There he saw Riley in her skin-tight jeans, straightening the plaid comforter. A thought rushed through his mind: Nick had sought and found someone just like his mother, a real pisser.

"Is he back?"

"He's in the kitchen with Gloria."

"Did she pounce on him?"

"Just about knocked him off his feet."

"Listen, Riley, I don't know if you'll tell me the truth or not, but," he tilted his head toward her, and ran his fingertips over the scar above his right eye, "is he clean?"

"Yeah. Sure."

"I can't tell the difference." He walked into the room and closed the door with the heel of his loafer. "Look, things are tough between us. Well, you know that. We rub each other the wrong way. I'm his father, and naturally I want the best for him."

"He really deep down loves you."

"Odd way of showing it, by drowning himself in drugs." He shrugged as though at a loss of what to say, and went to the window and looked out over Lincoln Center. Taxis pulled up to the curb, discharging passengers. The crowd was gathering for the afternoon matinee. For a second, he wondered if that nice woman, Irene, had found her purse.

Kevin turned and leaned back against the wall. "I know Nick's bright and intelligent and charming to boot."

"You're right about that."

"When he was a young kid, he'd play with a huge set of blocks and construct the highest buildings, and then stand back, show it off to whoever was around, then kick it down with a grin that stretched across his face. I didn't know whether his delight was in construction or demolition."

"Probably both."

"I expected he'd be an engineer, or an architect, or a builder, something tangible."

"Maybe your expectations were overwhelming?"

"I feel he's running away from something."

"Kevin! He's not running away." She stepped in close. "He's running toward you."

Kevin stepped back, avoiding the look of Riley's bare midriff. "Will you let me know if he gets in trouble or something?"

"Sure. Listen, is it really okay with you that we stay here?"

Stalling for a moment, he ran his hand along the window sill. "Yes, that'll be fine." He moved slowly across the room and opened the door. The smell of burned pastry filled the air. "Oh shit! The quiche."

In the kitchen, Kevin was met with the burnt crust of the flattened quiche sitting on the counter, while Gloria was busy pulling plates, flatware, and glasses from the cabinets. Nick sat on a bar stool, sipping orange juice from a champagne glass.

"Making yourselves right at home, I see." He regretted the noticeable edge to his voice.

"Kevin, don't be that way. We're family. Thick and thin, we're together again."

"Gloria, what the devil are you up to?"

"A shower and change." She wagged her finger toward Nick. "Move my luggage into the master bedroom." She took off the red beret and twirled it on her forefinger, then kissed Kevin on the cheek, a brief touch leaving a smudge of lipstick.

"Wait just a minute! This sudden—" He watched Nick slide off the barstool, and Gloria's trim body make her way toward the bedroom. Never had he felt quite so helpless. He loved her still.

CHAPTER SEVENTEEN

In the luxurious apartment on the seventh floor, things settled down by midnight. Gloria slept peacefully in the master bedroom, having made room for her wardrobe by pushing aside Kevin's belongings. Kevin, staring at the ceiling, lay awake on the sofa in his office. Riley, curled on her side in the guest bedroom, snoring softly like the purr of a kitten. Nick, however, tossed off the comforter, slipped from the bed, snuck into the dark of the kitchen, and foraged in the pantry for his long-hidden cache.

His arm reached to the back of the pull-out shelf, fingertips searching for the edge of the tape holding his stash. He knew this was against his better judgment, but his body moved forward as though he couldn't help himself, thinking, it's just a tiny little package, one pinch at best. Reaching further toward the back, his elbow brushed against small containers of spice, one knocking into the next as though fallen soldiers, tumbling and falling in a clatter of cymbals. He froze, listened for sounds of having roused someone.

Met with silence, he groped over the containers of flour and sugar and packages of cookies, certain that just one snort would help him sleep. His lips moved, forming the words, "I can quit anytime I want."

Nick stopped and thought of Riley's trust in him, and of group sessions in the sober home, the hooked vets, the homeless struggling, and the coffee, doughnuts, talk and talk and more talk. This was his second chance, maybe his third. He stepped back away from the pantry. His lips pinched closed. He knew he should talk to Riley. They supported each other.

Softly, he closed the pantry door, turned and saw the dark shape of his father in the kitchen. "Sorry if I woke you."

"I wasn't asleep."

"Oh."

Kevin flipped on the wall switch, the overhead light searing through the darkness. He opened the refrigerator and took out what was left of the ham, a hunk of cheese, and mustard. "You hungry? Want a sandwich?"

"I was, uh, was just looking for a cookie."

"You don't have to say that. I threw out that package last time you were here."

Nick nodded, and looked down at his hands. "I don't do it anymore. I'm really clean, well, all except a little pot."

"Just a momentary lapse?"

"No." He backed into the closed door of the refrigerator. "Yes."

The harsh overhead light shone on Kevin fiddling with the makings of two sandwiches. He took a knife and sliced into the ham, smeared mustard on the rolls, then slid a plate across the counter in front of Nick. "I'd like to keep an open mind with you."

"I had a couple of hits this afternoon. That's all."

"Is that going to drop you down the hole again?" Kevin wanted to shake the boy until his teeth rattled, smack some sense into him. Or maybe clutch him tight, shelter him, give him strength, give him the will to overcome his dreadful longing. But, instead of moving, Kevin just stood.

"I blame myself for being an absentee father."

"Yah. I didn't see much of you."

Kevin lifted the sandwich to his mouth, then looked at it, turned it over, and placed it back on the plate. "I'm guilty for stepping aside with no idea what was happening. Gloria took total control. She always said you were good, handsome, just out sowing your wild oats."

Nick fingered the top of the sandwich. Pursing his lips and pressing down onto the bread with the flat of his hand. Mustard squirted onto the counter top. He picked up the sandwich, took a nibble, and pushed the plate of ham and cheese away. He slumped over the bar stool, thinking his life had shredded into a meaningless piece nothingness. He was just hanging on each day.

"I was just a kid, doin' mischief. Gloria had no idea where I was or what I was doing. She was racing around with her own career." He shook his head at how easily it had happened, one misdeed leading to another. At thirteen, he had his first beer, and Gloria thought it was cute. By fourteen, he was good at rolling homegrown weed for her.

He sifted through the stages that had brought him down: surfing, drinking and skipping school with the older boys, taking money from Gloria's wallet, one misdeed leading to petty theft and drugs and panhandling and jail and the sober house he had fled.

Nick turned his head away, unable to face the man who had paid for his rehab both times and maybe, just maybe, still wanted to stick by him. He rocked back and forth as though soothing an infant with night terrors. His fingers suddenly gripped the edge of the counter, and he bent over. He felt as though he would burst open. He gripped the edge of the counter until his fingers were numb. "I've done some terrible things. I stole your bike."

"We'll work something out."

Nick straightened up while tears pooled and slowly streamed down the length of his face. Heart racing, he placed both palms face up on the counter. Sobbing, his voice croaking with the words, he said, "I need your help."

CHAPTER EIGHTEEN

Wallet secure in her leather tote, Irene waited until the guard unlocked the door to the bank and business hours had begun. A quick walk across the small lobby, she knocked on the glass partition of the manger's cubicle.

"Can I help you?" A woman in a pin-striped suit and red tie knotted perfectly sat erect behind the desk, reminding Irene of the severe principal of her high school.

Irene said, "Good morning." A smile stretched across her face grew even more ingratiating. "I have a little problem. The safe deposit key, well, I seem to have lost it."

"Weren't you given two when you first signed for your box?"

Irene stepped into the little office and sat on the visitor's chair. "I don't have it. I've lost it. Both of them."

The woman raised her chin in a dismissive manner. "Identification?"

Fumbling in the oversized tote, Irene pulled out her wallet. "Here, my driver's license. I need to get into my safe deposit box."

"Do you have an account here?"

"Oh, yes, in my husband's name, Ashford. Ashford Aubrey."

The woman's eyes shifted from the card to Irene and back again, then she typed on the computer's keyboard. She focused on the screen for a long moment, and tapped again. She pushed the license back across the neat desk to Irene. "There is no account here in his name."

"Really? Are you certain?"

"Absolutely."

"That's impossible. He has a large savings account with this bank."

"Ma'am! There is no account under the name Ashford Aubrey."

"There is no account? But—" Irene felt a shot of adrenaline attack her nerves.

"Mrs. Aubrey, are you sure the box is at this bank?"

Her hands shook, and she grasped them together to stop the trembling. "Did he close an account here?"

"I'm not at liberty to disclose any further information."

"But I'm his wife." Irene looked across the lobby toward the bank of tellers. A feeling of dread caused her stomach to turn with a rumble. She pulled the tote from the floor, placed the license back in her wallet, then clutched the bag to her chest. Her heart was thudding like the bass drum in the final scene of *Aida* when all is lost. She felt like a cliché, a divorcee without a clue to her husband's finances.

"I need to get into my safe deposit box. It's very important."

"And the lease is in your name?"

Irene's toes curled inside her loafers. "Yes. It's in my name."

Tapping again on the keyboard, the manager's fingers flew until finally she leaned back away from the computer screen, and pressed her hands together in the shape of a steeple. "Are you certain you can't find the keys."

Irene could feel herself shrink at the principal's reprimand. Her foot jiggled up and down, the tote was tightly clutched against her body, and she nodded to what seemed a scolding. Between clenched teeth she repeated, "They are lost."

"We'll have to drill the box open. Of course, you will be billed. Do you understand?"

"Of course, I understand."

Watching as though a slow-motion film, Irene saw the woman slowly get up from her chair, pull at the hem of her jacket. As though talking to an eight-year-old, she said, "I'll get the necessary paperwork. When your identification is verified, we will call the locksmith and coordinate an appointment."

"This morning?"

"Probably not."

"Please, make it happen today."

"If the schedule permits." The manager puffed up her breast like a rooster, and towered over Irene. "We will schedule a suitable time for the locksmith, witnesses, and you to be present. This is not simply a snap of fingers and your lock is opened. This will take time and effort." With that, the woman strode from the office.

"Please." She begged, "Please."

Back and forth, Irene paced in the cubicle. She hit her forehead with the palm of her hand. She had just used the same voice as when she was pleading with Ashford. With her husband, she knew her words went unheard. She should have stopped begging him, and this stern woman as well.

Biting on her lower lip, Irene felt the same sense of humiliation she had endured each Friday morning when Ashford tossed an envelope of money to cover household expenses on the kitchen table, never handing it to her. Sometimes he deliberately dropped the packet, and watched Irene grovel on the floor for the generous amount, a small portion of which she siphoned off as mad money and secreted in her safety deposit box in this bank.

Irene checked the clock on the wall behind the teller and drummed her fingers on the top of the woman's desk. Irene thought of her caring uncle, just the opposite of her husband's demeaning behavior. Her uncle was a kind and generous man taking her under his wing when she was in need. With this thought, her decision to end their marriage of long and arduous years was reinforced. She'd rather die like Aida than live another moment with Ashford.

She went to the door of the cubicle, searching for the woman. She had to get in the box today. It held more than cash. It held the key to her future.

CHAPTER NINETEEN

Kevin took a gulp of coffee, put on his cashmere sport jacket, grabbed his portfolio, and walked toward the private elevator where Gloria stood in a translucent peignoir, her cheek set as though awaiting a kiss good-bye.

"Kissee kissee."

"Gloria. We have to settle things."

"Course we do."

"Let me make it very clear. It's fine, actually more than fine, that Nick and Riley stay here for as long as they are both clean, and I mean squeaky clean. But you, you get your things out of my room and move to wherever you want. You cannot stay here."

"Oh, come on. Don't be mad."

"I mean it."

"You know this is simply a lovers' quarrel."

"After twenty-two years, you call this a quarrel?"

"Don't you see?"

"What I see is that once again you are thinking only of yourself. Honestly, Gloria, I'm tired of your games. It's time to grow up!"

Her emerald eyes softened, her voice lowered, and her sultry movements were not lost on Kevin. Despite himself, he felt an arousal.

"I've come back to you."

"No."

"Be happy now."

He thought he should be happy. He remembered following her around as though leashed as an adoring pet. Proud of being her husband, he wondered if she was ever proud of being his wife. He could not imagine what she had wanted from him so long ago, then or now. It was not likely she had willingly left all her professional contacts behind at this point in her career.

With one step toward the elevator, Kevin looked at the fine lines on her forehead and at the edges of her eyes, those age lines normally hidden behind makeup and the photographer's touchup. For a moment, he thought perhaps her glamour had faded, and she was no longer called by the agencies. Kevin had to admit that to him, she was still the beautiful young girl he had married. Time had not faded her glamour for him.

Gloria stood on tiptoe and kissed him on the ear. Her breath moist, she whispered, "Have a good day, dear. Dinner at seven."

At the close of the elevator doors, Gloria went back to the master bedroom and made order in the large closet, one side for her clothing, the other for Kevin's. She sorted, folded, and put his garments away in one drawer, her own flimsy lingerie in another. The triple dresser was the one she herself had chosen those many years ago.

Showered, dressed, and with full make-up applied, she walked down the hall and knocked on the closed guest room door. "Nick? Riley? Are you still here?"

"I'm in the living room." Riley called in answer.

Following the voice, Gloria's eyes flipped over Riley lounging on the white couch, the spiked hair perfect for the shape of her face, the cheek bones accentuated, the torso taut, the legs long and shapely, the bare feet narrow. "And what are you up to today?"

"Just hangin' out. Nick's out. He has an appointment. An interview, for a job."

"That's good.

"I'll get a job soon."

"Doing?"

"Sales."

"Experience?"

Riley sat up, her movement abrupt. "Geez, Gloria, I didn't expect to be cross-examined."

Gloria chuckled, and looked down her nose at the young woman, so full of youth and fresh ideas. "Can't blame me for being curious. After all, you're here with my son in this apartment."

"Not for long."

"Oh? What's your plans?"

"After we get jobs, then we'll move to our own place. Someplace Nick likes. Downtown for sure. Where the action is."

Gloria sat on the edge of the couch and crossed her legs. "You could model if you wanted. Like me."

"Me? You're kidding. I mean, look at you. You're gorgeous and beautiful. Me? I'm not anything to look at."

"True, the camera loves me." The map of Gloria's face changed as she struck a pose, her lips pursed, her chin angled. The demeanor took on that of an enchantress, shy at first, shifting to alluring, all within a fraction of a moment. The very blonde hair fell as a wave over one raised shoulder. "It's an intimate relationship. The camera and I, we love each other. I can do the same for you."

"You're kidding me."

"Just the right touch is needed."

"You're serious?"

"Perfectly. You have good features."

"That won't get me very far."

"I'll apply a little magic."

Riley lifted first one foot off the Oriental rug, then the other, and pulled her knees close to her chest, her bare thighs gripped in her crossed arms. Her chin rested on her knees, and with her eyes closed she asked, "And?"

"I know the right people to make it happen."

"You make this sound so easy."

"It's hard work, but I'm sure we can make this happen."

"What's the downside of this?"

"You'll do what I say. Night and day, if necessary."

"Just what do you have in mind?"

"Just so we're clear with each other. You are to stay here with Nick in this apartment, and do whatever I ask of you."

Riley nodded like a hand puppet, one eyebrow raised. "I'd be your slave? Is that it?"

"Coarse way of saying it. Yes."

"The model part sounds good."

Gloria pushed herself up from the couch and sauntered to the window side of the living room. She looked out to the street below, the cars whizzing past, people scurrying across the plaza. Then her focus switched and swept the living room; the two canvases, a Chagall over the fireplace and a known Picasso of horse and boy, the black Steinway baby grand. Her eyes wandered as though placing a dollar sign on each item readying for an auction. Finally, her eyes came to rest on Riley. "And your answer?"

"It's against my nature."

"Is that a no or yes?"

CHAPTER TWENTY

Irene brought a tissue to her nose, the smell of oil potent in the cave of safe deposit boxes. With the armed guard, the severe bank official, and the witness, the locksmith finished his task by putting away his drill. Irene pulled the safe deposit box from the shiny wall. The heavy box held in her arms, she retreated to the tiny room affording her privacy. She lifted the top of the metal box and pulled out the first of many papers. Here were the copies she had made of the many documents Ashford had kept in his locked desk drawers.

One after another she scanned trusts and wills of people unknown to her. The forms were all signed and notarized, giving Ashford Power of Attorney, trustee to their wills and authority to further transactions. Irene couldn't imagine all these people putting total reliance in her husband. Toward the bottom of the pile, she found one with her name as principal. She had no memory of ever signing this form, nor was it her authentic signature.

It took her a while to count all the one hundred-dollar bills accumulated. Midway she lost count. She started again, and made piles by the thousands. Her fingertips turned black, her mouth was dry. Stuffing the cash, the few pieces of jewelry also secreted in the box, and the bundles of papers into large manila envelopes, she left the bank with the tote dragging down her left shoulder.

A cab responded immediately to signal, pulled up to the curb and she slid onto the torn vinyl seat. Her voice shook, and her throat closed on the Madison Avenue address of her attorney. The cab headed west, then north through mid-town traffic.

Waves of office workers plowed from the buildings at lunch time and overflowed the sidewalk. A jaywalker banged on the hood of the cab. Irene flinched. She scanned the cars alongside, watched the pedestrians crossing too closely to the cab's door. Swiveling on the seat, she checked the cars directly behind. She wanted to get out of the cab and push the trucks that were double parked, the obstacles to her destination. Her cotton turtle neck top was tight at her neck, the jacket overly warm. She was hot and cold at the same time.

Finally, they arrived. Irene paid the driver and stepped from the cab, jostled by the crowd emptying from the building, the armies of clerks and secretaries and professionals streaming in the opposite direction. A homeless man pushing an overflowing shopping cart brushed her side and Irene panicked, tripping over her own feet. Her fingers numb, she entered the sleek office building, and edged her way into a packed elevator.

The air was thick with the smell of perfume and sweat. Squashed in the small space of the moving cell, Irene was jostled as the doors opened and closed at each floor. She pressed herself to the back corner, her eyes soaking up those surrounding her, the tote held tight against her chest. Wary as a nervous rabbit, Irene twitched when an arm or a shoulder touched her. A pool of sweat collected under her armpits. She wondered why sane people would subject themselves to this ill-treatment day in and day out. At the thirteenth floor, Irene pushed her way to the front and out of the elevator. Thinking of thirteen as a bad omen, she followed the directions down the hallway.

It took but a few strides to cross to the heavy glass doors and enter the quiet space of the attorney's offices. The carpet was thick under her loafers. Walls of books lined one wall. Beyond the leather couches, arm chairs, and coffee table stacked with magazines, was the receptionist, an officious elderly woman. Irene stood for a moment, immobilized, and yet relieved by the finality of at long last divorcing Ashford, and the wreckage of her marriage.

"Can I help you?"

"I have an appointment with Mr. Block."

"And you are?"

"Irene Aubrey"

"Oh, Mrs. Aubrey, one moment please." The receptionist pushed a few buttons on the phone system, announced Irene's arrival, then nodded, "It'll be just a moment. Please make yourself comfortable."

Irene almost laughed, trying to remember the last time she was comfortable. Too agitated to sit down, she went over to the wall of books. Her eyes flitted from one end to the other, barely seeing the titles. She moved to other side of the room, where a huge old dictionary lay open on a wooden stand. A quick glance at the receptionist, Irene shifted the weight of the tote to her other hip, then leaned against the back of the couch.

"Will he be much longer?"

"Pardon?"

"I said will Mr. Block be much longer?"

"Another moment, Mrs. Aubrey."

Gripping the tote, Irene took a seat on one of the arm chairs. She perched on the edge while holding the tote tightly on her lap. Reaching for a magazine, she opened it at random, shuffled through a couple of pages, and placed it back on the stack. Her eyes closed, she took a large gulp of air, and began counting backwards from one-hundred.

A hand tapped Irene on her shoulder, and she lunged away, bumping wildly into the table.

"I'm so sorry, Mrs. Aubrey. I didn't mean to startle you."

Every muscle in her body contracted. Her heart raced. She coughed to catch hold of herself. "I'm a bit nervous."

"I'm sorry I surprised you. I'm Mr. Block's secretary. I've tried to reach your cell. I've left several messages."

"It's in the bottom of my bag."

"Mr. Block had a family emergency, and had to cancel your appointment."

"He's not here?"

"Would you like to reschedule?"

Irene indicated the tote. "I have some documents for him."

"You can leave them with me."

"No! No, I can't. When will he be back?"

"I really can't say."

"You must have some idea!"

"Shall we reschedule?"

Irene focused on the flickering of the secretary's dark eyes, the shifting of her feet, and fingers entwined in nervous hands, and wondered if Ashford had something to do with this delay. "If you don't know when he'll be back, how can you reschedule this appointment?"

"I'm certain next week or the week after will be fine."

Feeling the need to kick and scream, Irene stood like a pit bull, her jaw clamped shut, biting down on every scrap of self-control. She was rigid as a granite statue, not letting go until she broke loose, picked up a magazine and slammed it on the table. "No! I will not reschedule."

Irene turned and moved across the carpet as though in flight. Out of the glass doors, into the hall she punched the down button for the elevator and waited, gripping her worldly possessions, eager to flee the bad-luck thirteenth floor.

She paced back and forth until the elevator whisked her down to the lobby. Snatches of conversations bounced off the stone floor and soared high to the ceiling. Overcome with the sensation that life was moving too quickly and at the same time, creeping along slow as a sloth, she stopped mid-step, sighting a somewhat familiar face.

She ducked her head, and turned to the directory of tenants and scanned the names. From the corner of her eye, she saw the man was striding directly in her direction. Looking for an exit, she whipped around so abruptly, the heavy tote slid off her shoulder, the manila envelopes sliding out onto the marble floor. Irene crouched to retrieve the documents.

The man bent down beside her. "Irene? Right?"

She ransacked her brain to remember his name. "And you're the man who hums Aida's melody."

"Ah, you remember. Kevin's the name."

"You were very kind to me, a stranger."

There was a twinkle in his eyes as he placed his hand on her elbow. "That sounds like a film with Marlon Brando. Be careful, young lady, you're dating yourself."

Irene laughed at the reference. She picked up her bag and hefted it back onto her shoulder. "It's the kindness of strangers that come at the most unexpected moments."

CHAPTER TWENTY-ONE

Kevin watched as Irene left the building. The sight of her orange jacket was lost in a crowd of tourists following a guide's small red flag held aloft. He marveled at the smallness of the big city, full of skyscrapers and big ideas. Everyone was important in their own way, like the spokes of a wheel supporting the wagon.

He walked west on 57th Street, admiring high-end designers' boutiques lining the thoroughfare, the window displays of Chanel, Saint Laurent, and others had been unnoticed on his daily bike rides to and from the office. Too concerned with traffic, he'd ignored the shiny glass facades of the newest buildings.

Feeling as though the city had grown up without his knowledge, he slowed his pace and stopped in front of Tourneau's window filled with men's and women's watches, crossed the street to Bergdorf Goodman, and entered the glamorous atmosphere. Instantly, he was overwhelmed by the aroma, the fragrance of his mother's perfume, and of the many shopping sprees he had been forced to join. This was a place his mother had frequented, and he hesitated as though he was again holding her hand, listening to her voice.

"This is hallowed ground." She'd bent low and adjusted his schoolboy uniform, the navy jacket and white shirt. "Here your taste will be refined. Today we'll start with the jewelry. Look carefully."

"I've got homework. Can't we go home?"

"Don't be childish. This is a life lesson."

Trailing his hand over the showcases filled with multi-colored gems, his fingertips left smears along the glass. The man behind the locked case shook his head, and Kevin shrank back against his mother's knees.

His mother wiped the sticky candy off his hand with a lace handkerchief, and marched him to the next case. "Stand up straight."

"I am."

"Now, can you pick your favorite?"

"I don't know," he twisted his tie around his hand.

"Stop shrugging."

His eyes closed, he pointed. "Maybe this one?"

"Kevin, this is not pin the tail on the donkey."

"Mom."

She bent down, grasped his shoulders, and shook him. Then she straightened his jacket and smoothed her palms along his face. "I want you to start behaving like the young man of privilege that you are. School teaches you reading and writing and arithmetic, but it is my job and obligation as your mother to introduce you to the finer things in life." She stood. "Now, just pretend every colored stone is a gum drop, and choose one for me."

As he grew older, she demanded he escort her once a week to either a museum, a concert, the opera, or a ballet. She called him her "prince among men" and made certain that he wanted for nothing and that life would be good for him. What he did want was to be chosen on a team, play baseball, and go to the soccer field with the kids.

"Mom, please, I told them I'd be there."

"Sorry, dear. Today we are going to the planetarium. You'll be glad once we get there."

"But my friends are waiting for me."

"You'll thank me when you grow older."

Quite lost in the memories of his mother, Kevin's fingertips ran along the glass displays as he meandered, recalling the manner in which she had nurtured and carefully sculpted him. As a youngster growing up, he had wanted wings, some magical way to set him free of the constant restraints of his mother's strong will. It was in this very store that she had modeled one sparkling necklace after another, had pointed to glistening displays of diamonds and rubies, had slipped bejeweled bracelets up and down her wrist.

Looking back, he appreciated all his mother had done for him, but what he had really wanted all those years ago was to be part of a team, play ball with the other kids. And what he truly craved was to go to sleep-away camp with the other kids. He finally got his wish, but only after she had died.

Kevin stopped, mid-step, the loss raw and fresh in his memory, a hole waiting to be filled.

A dignified salesman stood at the ready, asking, "May I be of assistance?"

He indicated with the tip of his head, "Those earrings are beautiful."

"They belong on a special person."

"You're right about that."

CHAPTER TWENTY-TWO

At the stroke of seven, Kevin rode the elevator to his home on the seventh floor. He strode across the marble entry and into his foyer, following the scent of garlic into the kitchen. Counter tops were laden with covered dishes, steam rose from a large pot, and a waiter stood, white linen napkin over his forearm.

"Good evening, Sir."

"Who are you?"

The waiter tipped his head, his jet-black hair licked back. "Angelo, Sir, from Lincoln Restaurant."

"What's all this?"

"We've prepared a fine dinner for your family this evening."

"Gloria," he yelled storming down the hall. "What the hell—"

"Darling," Gloria came sweeping out of the master bedroom. "Don't get yourself all out of kilter. I didn't hear you come in. I was just going to make certain all is as I've planned for us." She hugged his stiff body, then leaned back, looking directly in his eyes. "It's from our special restaurant, you know, from when I was pregnant. Do you remember?"

"I do." For an instant, he remembered mumbling those words while staring into her eyes with the expectation of a long life of togetherness. He couldn't resist her then. He was the clay she molded to suit her own purposes.

"Now the whole family can sit down together and enjoy." She knocked on the guest room door, "Nick, Riley, we're ready for dinner."

In the dining room, the table had been set with Kevin's finest ancestral china and silver, with Austrian crystal wine glasses glinting from the overhead pin lights. The elegant centerpiece resembled a wedding bouquet, dripping with a mix of fresh flowers, roses, hydrangea, lilies, and pale dahlias all spilling from the vase onto the lace table cloth.

Nick held the chair for his mother to be seated. "Thank you, dear." Kevin, likewise, seated Riley. Gloria took the little silver bell and lifted it for the tinkled sound "I've suggested a wonderful menu."

The waiter entered as though on stage. His voice was deep, and the Italian accent sounded well practiced. "The appetizer this evening is Polpo Alla Griglia."

Kevin's fingers drummed on the table. "What is that?"

"Grilled Octopus, Nebrodini Mushroom, Fresno Pepper, Charred Lemon-Black Garlic Puree, Sir."

"Goodness," said Riley, looking down at the plate being set before her, "I've never had anything like this. Does it always come with such a good-looking waiter?" she laughed toward the efficient and handsome man, and moved slightly, a gesture to allow the thin strap of her camisole to reveal her cleavage. "You make the dish look very enticing."

Gloria picked up her fork. "You're referring to the dish in front of you, or the one serving?"

Nick laughed at the undertone. "Just a taste, Riley."

"I'll try anything once. Cross my heart, I promise I won't take a big bite."

Nick glanced at his mother. "She's not always careful."

Kevin was beginning to enjoy the growing feeling of family, and the possibilities it might bring. Watching Nick look at Riley with adoration in his eyes, the set of his lips forming a smile, the subtle lift of his chin, a feeling of comfort swept over Kevin. He stared at the young couple and wondered if their relationship would last.

Taking a first bite, he let the taste of the appetizer linger, allowing the sauce to rest on his tongue, enjoying the intense flavor before swallowing. He lifted the empty goblet toward Gloria, who motioned to the waiter. Immediately, the chilled Chablis was uncorked and poured by the efficient waiter.

Gloria rose, the silver lame sheath outlining her sensuous curves. "To my Kevin, a toast. You have always been in my heart. Not a precious day has gone by that you were not in my thoughts. I thought about you as I poured morning coffee, stood under heated lights striking poses. You have always been on my mind. And now at long last, we are together again." Her eyes sparkled as she slithered and settled in her chair.

Kevin sipped the fine wine and lowered his glass. "Your toast sounded very close to the lyrics of a Sondheim song. You should have given him credit. Nonetheless, I must admit, it's very pleasant to have Nick and Riley here tonight, and for that I thank you."

Riley reached across the table and took Nick's hand in her own. "And speaking for both Nick and myself, we are so very grateful to you for allowing us to stay here for a while."

"Only a short time," interrupted Nick. "We want to get a place of our own downtown, maybe the Village, or Soho."

Riley gave his hand a slight squeeze. "We decided, didn't we, that first we'll get jobs, and then we'll get an apartment."

Gloria placed her hands on the table. "I have great news. I've been on the phone almost the entire day working my magic. It took a great deal of my ingenuity. It's a fabulous surprise. I cannot imagine how I was able to pull it off, but I did." She cleared her throat. "Here goes. It's so exciting. I just know you'll all be thrilled. I got a call just before dinner."

Kevin shifted in his chair. "Gloria, what are you up to?"

"Come on, Mom, spit it out."

"Riley has an appointment tomorrow morning with my agency."

"Really?" Riley's hands raced to her cheeks. "Modeling?" Her voice rose to a high register.

"Modeling, of course."

"That's so great! Isn't that the tops, Nick? I'm going to be a model."

Nick leaned forward. A frown wrinkled his forehead in two vertical creases. He raised his shoulders in bewilderment and asked, "Are you following in my mother's footsteps?"

CHAPTER TWENTY-THREE

Not wanting to be burdensome in Julia's one-bedroom apartment, Irene unpacked just a few essential items, and moved the empty suitcase into the coat closet along with her tote, which still held the many papers from Ashford's locked desk. The cash had been divided, accounts opened and placed in various banks, leaving just enough in her wallet for day-time expenses.

Irene sank into the soft tufts of the arm chair, removed her loafers, and sat back. "At least that's done. A relief. It's amazing, the weight I carried around this afternoon."

Julia handed Irene a tall glass of iced tea, a slice of lemon dangling off the rim. "You are talking literally?"

"Yup, and all the papers, I can't wait to unload them tomorrow at your attorney's office. I hope to heaven Ashford doesn't have this attorney in his pocket as well."

"Even though he doesn't handle divorce cases, he'll be able to guide you to the right people. He's such a good guy. You'll like him, everyone does. Oh, wait, I have a photo of him from a rehearsal."

Opening the trunk which served as a coffee table, Julia hunted through piles of photographs and memorabilia while continuing to talk. "He plays a mean clarinet. Oh, I can't wait for you to join us. You'll have so much fun. We've become like, more than friends, more like a family. Ah, here we are." She handed the photograph to Irene.

Irene scanned the photograph of three men and Julia taken some years ago. She was much thinner and had a totally different hairdo. "Which one is he?"

"Henry's the tall one standing next to me. He got married last year."

"Were you a 'thing'?"

"For a short while. Too little time for anything to develop, or anyone to notice. I'm actually glad for him. He married this fabulous woman who plays the harp."

Irene couldn't help but notice the warble in Julia's voice. "Who's standing on the other side of you?"

"That's Kevin. He doesn't come that often. Terrific guy. And the other one in the back, he's no longer with us. Moved to Colorado."

"I know him. I mean the other guy, Kevin. I've met him." Her eyes on the photo, she brought it closer for a better look.

"You're kidding! For heaven's sake."

"It's a small world story. He's the man on the old bike I told you about. at Lincoln Center. He's the guy who I thought was homeless. Just this afternoon, I saw him again when I was leaving the office building."

"You might see him tomorrow night at rehearsal. Plays the guitar. Classical guitar." She tipped her glass toward Irene. "He's very charitable, and I believe he's single. You should get to know him."

"Oh my God, Julia, I'm not even over one hump, and you have me diving into another."

"Who can say what will happen?"

Irene leaned forward, her elbows digging into her thighs, her forehead cupped in her palms. "Here I am, thirty-six and I have never lived by myself. First it was my parents, and then I was lucky my uncle stepped in. In college, there were my roommates, and after graduation, I had more roommates. And then I jumped right into Ashford's arms."

"So? Now you'll stand on your own two feet."

"Honestly, I feel like I'm treading water. I'm just flapping around."

"I hope you don't have the nerve to feel sorry for yourself." Julia grabbed the glasses, strode into the little kitchen, and dumped the melted ice into the sink. She turned around, took a step, and faced Irene. "You have everything going for you, and that's the last time I want to hear you moaning." She leaned across the breakfast counter. "We're friends. We've been friends for years. Girlfriends, and we grew into women friends, and I know you'll do great."

"I feel so stupid."

"Don't you dare get stuck in a mire of self-pity. Once you speak to my attorney, you'll know what the next step is. Then it won't feel so devastating. Just take it one day at a time, one challenge at a time. You'll do fine. Now, come help me put together dinner."

Irene moved into the kitchen and opened the refrigerator. "Obviously, this is the refrigerator of a dieting single woman. There's nothing to eat in here."

"Just pull out the lettuce and don't make fun of me. I'm trying this new diet. It may prove to be my undoing."

"Okay. Take your own advice. One day at a time."

After a light dinner of a mixed green salad sprinkled with a can of water-packed tuna fish, Julia said good-night and went to her bedroom. Clear sounds of the flute traveled through the thin walls of the apartment. The major C scale floated, airy and clear. Settled on the living room couch, Irene listened to the rich, silvery hum of her friend's practicing, and without thinking about it, began to move her fingers up and down the scale of an imaginary piano. She leaned back, closed her eyes, and played the opening notes of "Rhapsody in Blue."

Later, when all was quiet, and the shades drawn closed, Irene flipped off the lamps and crawled onto the hastily made bed, covering herself with the white comforter. Staring into the dark, she turned from one side to the other, thinking of her narrow bed in the musty house of her childhood, the peeling blue and grey checked wallpaper of her little room, the low water-stained ceiling, and though she tried to block it out, she heard the incessant battles between her mother and father. Toilet paper stuffed in her ears did not help.

Restless through all the sounds of the night, she heard the dripping water faucet in the bathroom, the buzzing electric wire outside her window, the cars rumbling, and the thunderous voices of her parents' constant arguments. She'd not been able to ignore the persistent night sounds. But one night she fell into a deep sleep: a sleep so cavernous the crackling did not waken her as smoke and fire swept from the kitchen through the downstairs and curled up to her room. She only woke when the fireman grabbed her. Shivering in her nightie, she stood barefoot on the cold ground, and watched as the little house became a glowing ember, tongues of fire leaping into the night sky, turning her parents to ash. It was the end of her childhood.

CHAPTER TWENTY-FOUR

There was nothing special in the spare room. Head shots, full face, profile, top to toe photographs, Riley stood in front of the white screen, turning this way and that as directed. Not accustomed to following instructions, the shoot was more irritating than tiring, and not at all as Riley had imagined. There were no special spot lights, no assistants running around, no extensive lenses, only the sound of a trumpet played in the background, while a man behind a simple camera issued instructions.

"Okay, no smiles. Just wave at something you long for."

Obediently, Riley responded.

"Give me yearning."

Riley swallowed and gritted her teeth, reminding herself she was merely a puppet following a man's instructions.

"No. No! Too studied. Give me coy."

She twisted and looked over her shoulder, her eyes burning with disdain.

"Try something seductive."

Curling, she coiled, her tongue licking her upper lip.

"Give me something wild, something over the top."

Her arm lifted in a balletic pose, she wiggled her wrist as though a sarcastic answer to the request.

"That's not responsive," the voice said out of the side of his mouth to Gloria. "She's nothing special."

Gloria leaned over the man. "Let her do her own thing. Riley, go for it."

Just as Gloria had suggested, Riley put her thumbs inside the waist of her shorts and pushed them down with the ease of a snake ridding its skin, her eyes never flickering from the eye of the camera. The moment became Nick and the first time she'd seduced him back, at the rehab, sneaking off to the lake, stripping, diving, and luxuriating in the cool waters. She'd grasped Nick with her long limbs wrapped around his body, and in her greed and hunger, ravaged him. He was hers to own. The beatings she'd endured were forgotten, pushed to the furthest hidden valley in her brain, buried, masked, with Nick and Gloria and Kevin as her protectors, or so she'd like to think.

"Turn. Let yourself go."

The session proceeded as Riley removed each article of clothing, the last piece the flimsy black lace thong removed with dignity, her head held high in self-pride, her middle finger raised in a "fuck you" pose.

Later, Gloria and Riley sat as the photographs one by one were splashed on a screen, starting with coy and ending with seduction and her final gesture.

Riley watched the model on the screen, as though seeing someone else, and when the last photograph was shown, she laughed. "Well, at least that's truly me."

Gloria crossed her legs and turned her focus to the man behind the projector. "Told you Riley's a natural."

CHAPTER TWENTY-FIVE

By the time Julia and Irene arrived at the auditorium, a few of the community musicians had already placed their music stands and scores on the stage of the private school. Greeting one another with handshakes and hugs, Julia introduced Irene, saying, "She's a very fine pianist. So, if we ever need an understudy, she's willing. Right?"

Irene placed a palm on her chest. "I'm just here to listen."

"Don't let her fool you. Classical, pop, jazz, whatever, she's spot on."

"I'm not certain I can live up to that, but thank you."

The drummer played a roll. "Professional or amateur, talent's always welcome here."

Taking their places on stage, the musicians took instruments from cases, unfolded chairs, set up music stands, and turned their music scores to the first piece. There was something intimate about the group, as though they knew each other's strengths and failings, the strong helping the weak.

Irene sat listening to the tune-up. All instruments tuned to the oboist's pitch of "A." Though there existed an electronic device which could be used to sound the tuning note, Irene was pleased that these musicians stayed with the original sweet and clear sound of an oboe. A few latecomers straggled in, opened their cases, jumped onto the stage, and took their seats.

The first violinist tapped on his stand for quiet, and Irene watched as the musicians—both the skilled and the novice—raised their eyes to the conductor. She longed to sit on the piano bench amongst these eager musicians, and give her undivided attention to the balding man with the baton.

With a wave of his arm, the orchestra dove headlong into Howard Hanson's *Symphony No. 2*. The contemporary piece, an ambitious undertaking, had a seductive charm, with a slow build of intensity, the theme pressed down with dark and mysterious currents, reminding Irene of the funeral march in *Aida*. Pushed away were thoughts of Ashford, the stack of documents, the secreted cash, as the music filled her.

The conductor wiped his bald pate. "Better. Getting better. Yes. Think crisp. The audience will love this symphony." Applauding the conductor, the musicians packed away their instruments, folded chairs and music stands, and stacked them in the wings. Some jumped from the stage, while others sauntered down the few steps, leaving Julia alone on the empty stage with her flute.

It was then that Irene noticed Kevin, standing in back of the auditorium, remove a guitar from its case and walk toward the stage. He nodded as he passed by Irene, mounted the stage, unfolded a chair, and sat, cradling his guitar like a beloved child. With a few words of greeting, Julia lifted the flute to her mouth, Kevin fingered the strings, and a tango flooded the air. The music, written for flute and guitar by Piazolla, was never coy or pensive, but persuasive in the elegance of its tempos.

Wrapped in the pulse of this music, Irene tapped the mesmerizing rhythm, her feet moving until she could not sit still, but bolted up from her seat and danced to the sensuous beat. For Irene, it was over too soon. Clapping loudly, her applause echoed off the walls. "Wonderful," she shouted at the top of her voice. "Julia, oh my God, you are splendid, fabulous, and that guitar, fantastic. Oh my. Wow!" Her words kept jumping a tumble one over the other, as though she had so many thoughts, her actual words did not cooperate with her thinking. She patted her chest as though to catch her breath.

Julia pointed her flute toward where Irene stood. "That's my friend, Irene."

"We've met. Nice to see you again." Kevin turned to Julia, his smile a sign of a good job, and kissed her cheek. "Proud of you. You were absolutely on pitch, with clarity and excitement."

Julia licked her lips. "That was so good. We've never played so perfectly before. Could we ever do that well again?" She laughed, "Or was this a once in a lifetime event?"

Standing at the edge of the stage, Irene looked up at them. "I'm so overwhelmed by both of you. What a privilege to hear you guys. Did you see? I couldn't stay in my seat. You both… What a performance. It was bold and brilliant, the undercurrents of a… of a… I don't know, it was disturbing and radiant all at the same time. That tango swept me off my chair." A dreamy look softened the angles of her face. She placed both palms on her warm cheeks, cooling the sudden flush.

A door closed at the back of the auditorium. A custodian with a long broom came down the aisle. "I gotta be closing."

"That's our cue." Kevin jumped off the stage and shook Irene's hand. His grip was strong and powerful, his long and elegant fingers had calluses at the tips.

There was a lilt in Julia's voice when she called out. "Wait, Kevin! Wanna join us for a drink?"

Kevin nodded. "Sounds good."

Irene glanced from one to the other. Her thumb played with the empty space on her ring finger. The duet they performed had been spiced with a controlled passion. Irene certainly did not want to be the third wheel. "You two go on ahead."

"No! No! Join us." Julia closed her flute case with a snap, tucked it under her arm, and went down the few steps.

"I have a big day tomorrow. You know… the attorney."

"A divorce lawyer," Julia said to Kevin, shrugging as though an explanation had been necessary. "She has a lot on her plate right now. Needs to find a place to live and a job."

"Goodness, Julia, you've only left out my social security number."

Kevin chuckled.

"You've just told him all about me."

"Soon she'll be a divorcee."

Irene's lips twitched with the ache in the back of her throat. Hating the definition allotted to her state, she would not shrink from opportunities or challenges. She slung the strap of her pocketbook over her shoulder. "Okay," she said, "onward. Let's go!"

CHAPTER TWENTY-SIX

The café had a heavy wood bar behind which two bartenders were at the ready, and from the scattered tables and chairs came a quiet murmur of customers finishing dinner or having a quiet drink. Vintage posters hung on the walls. A black and red print by Rene Grauer titled "le Secret," was near the entrance, next to a well-known Andy Warhol, and all along the walls of the dimly lit restaurant were a series of fashion posters. The smell of chops and bourbon filled the air. The low ceiling was reminiscent of days long gone, one in which Irene wanted to hide herself in a cloak of forgetfulness.

Irene spotted a group off in the corner, deeply engrossed in whispered talk. Kevin suggested a table away from the bar, which a couple had just vacated, and Julia excused herself to the ladies room, leaving Irene and Kevin looking at one another across the small table.

A waiter approached, a crisp white apron tied around his girth.

Kevin asked, "What would you like?"

"A Black Russian for me, and a vodka martini for Julia."

"I'll have a single-malt, Oban, if you have it. Neat."

The bar itself curved around toward the back of the restaurant, where in an alcove, a piano stood unattended. Irene motioned toward the vacant space. "I would venture to guess the music may be less important to this establishment than the drinks from the bar. This place has a 1920s' speakeasy old world feeling. Your drink may not be a single-malt."

Kevin sat back, a quizzical look on his face. "Why do you say that?"

"I know the bar business. My uncle worked in a place just like this."

"And?"

Her eyes wandered toward the rest room, as though urging Julia to return. "And… my uncle raised me from the time I was eleven years old. He passed away, but not before he paid for my college education. He taught me think of the less fortunate, and to lend a hand to the suffering. At the holidays, we'd set a long table with platters of food and feed the homeless. He couldn't tolerate any waste: food, time or talent." She leaned forward. "He was a good man."

The drinks were delivered just as Julia came back to the table and sat down. She lifted her glass, spilling a few drops from the wide lip. "To more tangos." She took a long sip, and placed the glass back on the table.

"I'll second that."

"Me too."

"So, what did I miss?"

"Kevin's been grilling me."

"Hardly."

Julia cleared her throat as though to make an announcement. "If he hasn't told you anything about himself, that's par for the course. He rarely discloses any pertinent info about his own life." She leaned toward Kevin, impersonating a police interview. "Thus far, all we know about you is a sketch: plays a mean classical guitar, not married, and lives alone. It's time, Mr. Brooks for you to fill in the blanks."

He nodded his head toward Irene. "First, I'm not alone right now. My son, Nick, and his girlfriend are staying with me for a while. My guitar and I manage styles beyond classical and further—"

"Julia, stop, you're embarrassing him."

"It's okay. There's not much to add, except," Kevin took a sip of his scotch, "Except I might be able to help you find an apartment."

"You're a real estate broker?"

"My God, no!" He fiddled with his drink, tapping his calloused fingers on the glass. "Sorry for the outburst, just not in the way you think of it. I have a management company."

Julia shook a finger as though continuing an interrogation. "All right, Mr. Brooks, now let's push ahead with your—"

"That's enough, Julia. Let the man enjoy his drink without these questions."

"That's okay, I don't mind. It's a simple question with a simple answer. It's not complicated. We oversee buildings and manage them. That's the long and short of it. Not exciting in the least."

"Maybe you can find a job for Irene. Like a package deal, a job and an apartment."

"Honest, Julia, please stop. This is so awkward." Irene swept up from the table and went to the dimly light alcove. Without a glance backward, she ran her fingertips lightly over the piano keys. Then with a soft touch she picked out the tune "Pennies From Heaven," tickling the keys with her right hand.

The hum of conversations died, the few remaining customers, alert to this unexpected sound. A fork was raised in midair, a waiter stopped busing a table, a bartender turned, a drink held and yet to be delivered. At this unanticipated musical entertainment, all eyes turned in Irene's direction, and though she felt a bit of stage-fright, she sat down on the piano bench and played a series of popular soft and sultry songs, and ended with her version of "New York, New York."

Julia grasped Kevin's forearm. "Told you she was good. Really, really good."

"She certainly is."

Irene mock-curtsied at the applause, and went back to the table, her cheeks flushed, her hair loose from the barrette. "Goodness, I don't know what came over me to do that. I'm usually so retiring. I've never done anything like that since my uncle passed away. It's not like me to just sit myself down and take over."

"I didn't know you were a professional."

"No, not at all. At one time, I played in my uncle's place. Now I play for my own enjoyment." Downing what was left of her drink, she said, "Time for me to go. You two stay."

"It's time for me, too." Kevin signaled for the check, and placed cash on the table. He ushered Irene and Julia out to the chilled night air and shrill sounds of the city, and said, "Perhaps I can find a piece written for flute, piano, and guitar. I imagine a contemporary composer must have written something."

Julia grabbed hold of Irene's arm. "We'd be an awesome trio. I'll practice until my lips swell. You will do it, Irene, won't you?"

"Count me out for now. You're forgetting, I don't have an instrument to carry around like you two. When I have an apartment, I'll get a piano, but for now it's a no-go."

Kevin's eyes rose to the street light. "You don't know of an available practice piano?"

"This whole separation divorce is brand new. Even though music has kept me sane all these years, it will have to take a back seat."

"I won't hear of it. No such thing as putting off music."

"Hopefully, it is only temporary." She held out her hand, saying, "Thanks for the drinks. Goodnight."

He nodded and stopped mid-step. "There's a baby grand just sitting in my apartment."

CHAPTER TWENTY-SEVEN

"...And so, I gave him the finger." Riley continued talking non-stop, tossed off the bedcovers, and climbed on top of Nick. "You should have seen the look on his face. There I was, standing all bare and sexy giving him the finger with a fuck you. Your Mom thought it showed my self-confidence, though she said I was a little brittle and she would have preferred I hadn't finished the shoot with that image. At least I finally got the photographer's attention."

Nick ran his palms over the inside of her bare thighs, the skin smooth under his touch, bringing him a renewed sense of longing. He filled his lungs to the fullest with the feeling of being taller and brighter with each moment shared with Riley.

"That's when I got him to look at me seriously. And I kept thinking of what else I could do. If I had a little help, even just a puff, I could have done something outrageous." She placed her hands on his shoulders and kissed his neck, her tongue licked under his chin until she sat back again on his thighs. "You know, a little weed won't hurt, once in a while. I'm happy to have a job, even if it is for a cheesy porn shot, but I know I could do better with a puff or two."

"Stop talking," he nibbled her ear.

"I thought you liked my voice."

"I love your voice."

She slipped her arms under his shoulders, and brought her breasts tight against his chest. Heat radiated off her in a slow burn. "How 'bout just a little joint between friends." Riley's hips moved in circles, barely touching Nick's groin.

"You're a tease," he said grinning under her touch, his body craving to be inside her.

"Wanna little taste?"

"No, I want it all. Every bit of it."

She arched her back and thrust her tiny breasts toward his mouth. "You can have it after a little puff."

"You're a tease." Grasping her waist, he pulled her down flat on his body. His wanting swelled as he pressed his hardness against her pelvis.

"One little puff and you can have all of me." She licked his nose. "That's all it takes," she murmured and nibbled his ear lobe, her voice husky with desire.

Nick ran his hands up her smooth thighs, and around her buttocks, opening an avenue.

Like a cat cleaning a newborn, she licked his lips and cheeks and the hollow under his chin. "You can't have me until I have what I want."

"Stop it." He pushed her off to the side of the bed and sat on the edge of the mattress, his head held in his hands. "What the hell is wrong with you?"

"What's wrong with me? God, Nick, just what the hell is wrong with you?"

He shook his head, every muscle in his body taut. "You have to stop doing that. We're together, remember, I promised you, I won't let it happen to you or me. If we fall into that pit again, I'll never be able to climb out."

Her lips tightened and her hands closed into fists. "You're right. You're right. Sorry. I got carried away, you know, with the modeling and stuff."

"I thought after you came to be with me, it would be different." His body drooped. "I wanted us to start fresh."

She snuggled up against him, wrapped her arms around his shoulders, and rested her head on his neck. "It's a new day. Don't be mad."

"I'm not." He looked over his shoulder at Riley. "We've got to help each other."

"You're strong, Nick. You'll figure it out for us both."

CHAPTER TWENTY-EIGHT

The attorney, Peter Sheehy, shuffled the papers strewn on his desk and looked over the top rim of his glasses, increasing his double chin and revealing dark shadows under his eyes. "Are you quite certain your marriage can not be salvaged?"

"I've been told that every divorce attorney asks the same question." Her back straight, Irene's voice did not waver. "My marriage to Ashford is positively over. Nothing on Earth will make me go back to living with him."

"Did he abuse you?"

A bitter laugh and Irene's body shuddered at the cruel taunts she had endured, the belittlement of her very being, the deceit of his not wanting children, the ordeal of his endless affairs. She'd almost believed that she was worthless and trapped, never able to resurrect her self-esteem. As though playing on a movie screen, one morning came to her mind. She remembered waking early. She'd slipped from under the down comforter, cautious not to wake Ashford, a light sleeper. She put on a silken robe over the matching nightgown, and crept down the creaking stairs, avoiding the loose fourth step.

As though on auto-pilot, she filled the percolator, set the table for one, sliced the whole wheat bread, poured the orange juice—careful not to let any pulp escape—and took a half-a-dozen eggs from the refrigerator. That morning was the beginning of the end. She felt the outside world tempting her to dare to leave him.

Irene could almost feel something happening deep under her flesh. She splashed cold water on her face and opened her mouth wide as the water streamed on her cheeks, wet her hair, ran into her ears, and splattered on her eyelids. She so wanted to feel something, have a sensation of living, if only for a moment.

With a dish towel, she dried her face, and tied the robe's silk sash in a tight knot around her tiny waist. She cracked first one egg, then another, and the next she crushed in her fist, letting the white leak between her fingers, the yellow yolk held captive for a moment.

The attorney asked again. "Did he abuse you?"

But Irene didn't hear the attorney. She was lost in the memory-film of Ashford's cruelty on that morning when she'd watched his every move, his fingers on the glass of juice, his Adams apple bouncing up and down as he swallowed, smeared butter on his toast, lifted a shiny silver fork full of dripping eggs. In this memory movie, she watched him finish his breakfast, wipe his mouth with the linen napkin and toss it aside to the floor. He pushed himself up from the table and moved close as she stood rigid before him, knowing what would come next.

He opened her robe and tossed it to the floor, flicking the straps of her nightgown to the side. He fondled her breasts, cradled first one and then the other, his thumb rough against her delicate skin. Suddenly, he shook her hard enough to make her bones rattle. And she remembered his voice, shrill and piercing in that early morning, "Christ, why on Earth did I ever marry you? You don't deserve to be my wife. You belong on a pig farm."

Irene remembered not even flinching. She had stayed still as the surface of a pond on a hot, humid summer day, the robe and nightgown pooled at her feet.

Shaking off all of Ashford, Irene looked straight at the attorney. "Verbally, if that counts."

"Grounds for divorce include cruel and inhuman treatment. Irreconcilable differences is one of the grounds under which a person may file for divorce. It generally means there is no hope that problems can be resolved and the marriage not saved." He tilted his head in a questioning fashion.

Irene's lips tightened as she nodded.

The attorney made a notation on a pad of paper. He sifted through a pile of documents until he held one in front of Irene. "And this is not your signature?"

"No. I never signed those papers. I'm not even sure why these trusts were ever written. When I saw them for the first time, I just thought something was not quite right. And then there were all those other names." She raised her shoulders. "I don't know who these people are. Ashford never discussed his clients with me. It's just, I thought it peculiar he'd bring these documents home and lock them in his drawer. Nothing made any sense. I knew asking Ashford to explain was futile."

Shifting her focus back across the desk to the elderly attorney, she continued, her eyes welling. "Perhaps I should blame myself for being stupid. I couldn't find a way to stand up for myself, and had no idea where the money came from or where it went, or even what we could or could not afford. I was blind. I can't say I did not enjoy the affluent life style, but when I saw those financial statements and tax stuff that just didn't seem to add up, and then that pre-nuptial paper that I never ever saw before, I made copies, thinking something just wasn't right, and someone would decipher it all for me. And then, finally, I thought they might help me get a divorce."

The attorney pushed a box of tissue toward Irene, and while she blotted her eyes and gathered herself, he called his secretary into the office. "Take these and make copies." He took off his glasses and placed them to the side. "You say your husband will not agree to a divorce."

"He said he'd never, never, never give me a divorce."

"We'll see about that, won't we?" He leaned back in his chair; hands clasped on his chest. "Give me a few days to review the documents you've delivered. In the meantime, make a full list of the marital assets. Everything, every dime, down to the last penny. I will inform Mr. Aubrey that you've hired me as your attorney and intend to proceed with or without his agreement."

"Do I have to talk to him?"

"All communication will come through me. If Mr. Aubrey is amenable to an Agreement of Separation, then we will proceed in that fashion with a legally binding contract laying out the terms and conditions of a divorce. A marital separation agreement does not have to be filed in court to be legally binding on both the husband and wife. The agreement is basically a contract between two people."

"He'll never agree to anything."

"After I have served notice, I'll request the name of his attorney."

Her lips pinched together, Irene drew a deep breath and lifted her chin. "He'll be defiant."

A strong ray of the late afternoon sun shined a beam on the full head of the attorney's snow-white hair. Irene leaned forward and pressed her fingers on the solid wood desk, her eyes travelling to the window past the attorney. Squinting against the glare, she could barely make out the skyline's silhouette. Off in the distance were the Chrysler Building, and the tall Empire State Building, all constructed on an island. As a bride, she'd thought her marriage would be just like those buildings, built on a strong foundation. Instead, it had not been well-built, but had wavered under Ashford's contempt, and crumbled as so much dust.

Her ice-cold fingers fumbled with her checkbook. Depleting her funds, she wrote a check for the retainer—three-thousand, five-hundred dollars —and handed it to the attorney.

"Divorce can be a very trying period. Trust that you're in good hands."

"Please, don't let this drag on. Ashford would like nothing better than to string this along and make me suffer."

CHAPTER TWENTY-NINE

Kevin thrust his hands into the pockets of his trousers, his gaze shifting from Gloria sitting on the edge of the couch to the windows where the setting sun had turned the sky into a kaleidoscope of color. He jiggled the loose change and keys in his pocket, as though to alleviate the quiver he felt run through his body. He swallowed back a tightening in his chest. He fingered the scar over his eyebrow, and stood watching the sky darken as Gloria rifled through pages of a fashion magazine, her long nails painted fire-engine red tapping on the glossy pages. Finally, he turned his back to the window.

"You can't stay here any longer."

"You don't mean that."

"And I mean you have to leave right now."

"Why are you talking nonsense?"

"I've been patient with this intrusion for long enough. It has got to stop."

"I can't believe you are saying this. You don't want me to be with you? Honestly, Kevin, you made all the overtures." She unfolded from her perch on the couch, went to his side, and slid her arm around his waist. "Making me give up everything and come back to be with you. I know you love me. We're so good together. Think of all the good times we had."

Listening to her sing-song voice, Kevin shook his head in disbelief, mumbling. "You're deluding yourself." He disentangled himself from her grip, strode across the room, and leaned against the piano. "Your idea of good is an endless delusion. You left me with the mere flick of an eyelash for a more chic lifestyle, a budding career, and an endless list of men."

"Darling, I've always loved you."

"I don't think you ever loved me."

"Do you remember the time—"

"Stop it, Gloria."

"I'd be in bed, warm and cozy—"

"That's enough. I've had quite enough."

She turned her back to Kevin. "Trust me, darling," her tantalizing voice turning icy, "I won't be alone for very long. I can just see you. You'll eat yourself up with jealousy."

Kevin ran his fingertips across the black ebony of the baby grand. He moved across the carpet and stood close to Gloria. He put his hands on her shoulders; his voice had a gentle quality, as though a smile was carried on its tone. "You were my very first and only love, and for years after you left, I was crushed." He turns her around to face him. "I guess some part of me will always love you. But, I have had enough. After all these years, I have to move on."

"I can be whatever you want."

"But I can't be what you want." He thought of his mother's manipulations, molding him into her ideal, the perfect little boy, the handsome teen, the top student, the clever business man. Her ambitions felt like a straitjacket. He could never be enough to fill her empty needs. "You're a survivor, Gloria, and it's true, you won't be alone for too long."

"And?"

"We just can't live together." He reached into his pocket and withdrew a set of keys. "I've made arrangements for you in one of my buildings. You'll like it there. A good number of business firms have apartments in the building. Very elegant, doorman, of course, and right off Madison."

CHAPTER THIRTY

Riley closed the tube of mascara, smoothed her eyebrows with the special wand, and applied a blue lip gloss. "That's better," she remarked to her image in the mirror.

"Talking to yourself?" Nick laughed as he shoved his arm into the windbreaker. He watched Riley slip her feet into ballet slippers, swish her long skirt, buckle a narrow-woven belt, and pull on a loose t-shirt cut short to end just under her breasts.

"Lookin' real hot."

Twirling, the skirt rose high to her hips, and she held her arms over head. "You like?"

He opened his arms and caught her against his chest. "You're going to love Ray's famous pizza. We should get there by eight. And afterwards, we'll window shop and wander, and maybe we'll go to a spot I know in the Village. A real great place with disco lights and—"

"Dancing! Great. If we're rocking it tonight, I have to change. Just give me a sec." She pulled out of his embrace, stepped out of the long skirt, kicked the ballet slippers under the bed, and reached across Nick.

"Riley, you were dressed fine. Whatever you wear, you look great,"

"I can't let anyone see me like that at a Club. Photographers are everywhere, and your Mom warned me to make sure I always looked the part."

"The part?"

She pecked him on the check. "You know, sexy."

"But I really liked the way you looked. I mean, we're just going to a pizza place and then maybe—"

"A club in the Village! We should skip the pizza."

"If that's what you want, but it doesn't really get started until midnight." As though he was an empty space, he watched her shuffle through the closet and the bureau until she'd found what she wanted; pink satin short shorts, argyle knee socks, her combat boots, and a tight lace turtle neck top with holes cut through the fabric, finishing off with the wide black belt wound twice around her tiny waist and clasped with a heavy gold buckle.

"Ta da! Now I'm ready."

"You'll need a jacket or something." He sounded like an old man to himself, worried about the weather, that she might get a chill, masking what he was truly worried about: the quick change in Riley. She was like a chameleon, her attitudes changing on a whim. He liked what she said and thought before she began following his mother around and being photographed in pornographic poses. Now he was not so sure. God, she was his girl. They were each other's support. She was going to need his protection from all the animals who would like nothing better than to maul her.

He went to the closet and removed her army jacket, holding it open for her. "You'll need this."

"Oh, don't be such a fuddy-duddy." Her nipples stiffened and poked through the lace like the pink nose of a pet mouse. Her glossy lips brushed Nick's check. "Let's go have fun!"

Down the elevator they held hands, Nick gazing with adoration, his head tilted toward Riley. "You're going to knock em dead."

"Think so?"

He tightened his grip on her hand. "Oh, yeah."

They stood at the corner until the light changed for them to cross the avenue. Heads turned toward Riley. The city was moving. A homeless man pushing his cart leered. A cat-whistle cut through the sound of cars rushing and the honking of horns. A stylish couple arm-in-arm walked past, the woman's eyebrows raised. A siren blared. Walking against the light was a group of teenagers encased in the familiar sweet aroma of marijuana. Riley "hi-fived" one of the teens.

Nick pulled Riley to his side and put a protective arm around her bare shoulders. "I need a pack of cigs."

"I need something more substantial."

Nick stopped, turned Riley to face him, and shook his head, "No. You don't need anything like that. We promised each other. You're my 'high' and I'm your rock. We're in this together. We're going to shake up the odds and make it. Right? We're clean."

Putting her arms around Nick, she pressed her body to his, lovingly tucked her hands into the back pockets of his jeans, and pulled out what was left of a joint.

CHAPTER THIRTY-ONE

"Yes, hello Mrs. Aubrey. Hold on, please."

Though Irene had steeled herself, her hand trembled like the wing of a hummingbird. She dropped her head, closed her eyes and quickly opened them, walked to the sink, poured a glass of water and set it on the counter, then paced from the little kitchen to the living room and back again to the kitchen, thinking that perhaps Ashford would agree to a Separation Agreement.

Though she'd been cautioned that all communications were to go through the attorney, she shifted the phone from one hand to the other, hoping that this, the third call to his office, would not end the same way as before.

"I'm sorry, Mr. Aubrey is unavailable."

"I'm fully aware Ashford won't take my calls, and I'm sorry you are being caught in this position of lying for him. Just give him this message. Tell my husband, he cannot avoid me forever."

"Certainly."

Irene picked up the glass of water and drank deeply. Next, she phoned her divorce attorney's office.

"Yes, Mrs. Aubrey. One moment, please."

Holding the phone away, Irene turned on the water faucet and refilled her glass. She sat on the counter stool and waited, her foot swinging back and forth. She glanced at the clock on the wall above the stove, and felt time was slipping away and she had accomplished nothing.

"Mrs. Aubrey. I'm sorry. Mr. Sheehy is in conference and cannot be disturbed."

"I've been trying to reach him all week."

"Yes, I know."

"Look. I don't know whose fault this is, but I need to move this forward. Mr. Sheehy has been unavailable, and I'm stuck here in a state of limbo." After a deep breath and a moment of silence, she added, "please tell him I need to speak to him."

Irene hung up the phone, her forehead wrinkled with the first twinges of a headache. It was as though a wall had been built surrounding her with immovable bricks, and her feet were encased in cement, stopping advancement in any direction. She pressed her fingertips on her scalp and massaged in slow circles easing the tension, swallowing each impasse with growing anger.

If she had been raised as an average child feeling this angry, she'd have stamped her feet, run outside, and kicked the dirt, or beat her fists against the wall, or cried on her friend's shoulder looking for sympathy and advice. But Irene had not had an average childhood. Like every little girl, Irene had dreamt of being a princess, being loved each day by adoring parents. Instead, she was belittled as "worthless." Massaging her forehead, she could hear her father's voice in her head: "You're good for nothing, just like your mother."

Irene had learned early in her life to hide hurt and anger deep inside, and retreat without a murmur, bury her emotions along with her mother. But now, walking into the living room, she tried to brush her past aside. Her first leap over the wall was leaving Ashford and all the trappings he afforded her. She'd miss the finery by turning her back on all that she'd left behind. Every muscle in her body wanted to race forward. But to take that next step without legal advice would be unwise. Ashford would probably sue her for abandonment. It was inevitable that he would stall the process until she was penniless and powerless expecting her to come crawling back to him.

Grabbing the *New York Times* from the coffee table, she tore open the real estate section. She sat on the edge of the couch, her feet flat on the floor, and once again scanned the ads for rental apartments. This time she saw there was a single possibility, a one-bedroom one-bathroom, rent-to-buy ad. Closing her eyes for a moment, she envisioned living in a small space all of her own. Did she dare to commit, take this next step without legal advice?

Irene circled the ad with a red fountain pen, the ink leaking onto her fingers, then ripped it from the paper, folded and placed it in her jacket pocket. Tomorrow she would look at the apartment. She wrote a quick note to Julia, grabbed her purse, and headed out for a quick errand.

Outside, she buttoned up her jacket against the wind whistling down the block, and headed east paying no attention to the slight drizzle. By the time Irene reached the corner, the tiny mist matured to a sudden downpour, drenching her as though she was standing under a cold-water faucet turned on full.

Huge puddles gathered. Cars splashed her. Irene raced across the street and ducked into the drug store. Catching her breath, she shook the water from her shoulders and wrung out her hair, spilling a stream of water onto the linoleum floor.

The clerk walked out from behind the counter with a floor sign which read, "slippery when wet." He placed it near the entrance.

A young couple bolted into the store, laughing and jostling one another in an intimate manner, and bumped into Irene, almost knocking her off balance. "Sorry, sorry," said the young man, who held out his hand in apology.

"My fault," said the young woman, brushing the skimpy blouse that clung to her body. "He didn't see you. He only has eyes for me."

The clerk ran a mop over the accumulating puddles from the dripping clothes. Then he dragged the display of umbrellas toward the front door.

"Some weather report, right Nick? And he gets paid for that bullshit. Maybe he's right fifty percent of the time. Isn't that right, Nick?" She nuzzled, closing in on his neck, then ruffled his hair and whispered in his ear. "I can almost smell the uppers in here."

"Riley, stop."

"Come on, Nick, loosen up." She ran her palms across her short shorts, then stomped her army boots and rolled her orange knee socks down. "At least my feet are dry. Doesn't look as though we'll get a cab in this monsoon. We might just as well settle in until it stops."

Irene went around the store until she found a rain hat, then went to the counter and waited for the clerk to return. Listening to the young couple, she thought she herself had once been young and wide-eyed and in love. Ashford! If only she'd been more careful, and they had talked, really talked. Perhaps if she'd seen the real Ashford, she never would have married him. He crept into her thoughts at odd times, and she wondered if she'd ever shake him off of her, wring him out. Once, she had stood quiet under his tirade and abuse, burying his words and actions. In the middle of their living room, she thought she'd like to put him in a garbage compressor and watch him come out as a tiny cube. Then she'd be free to tell him what she really thought.

A loud noise in the back of the store sounded as though a shelf of books had collapsed. In the overhead mirror Irene saw that a display and a shelf had been knocked over, the merchandise strewn down the aisle. She watched as the clerk and the young man bent to retrieve the display, while the young woman sprinted to the prescription department, and then reappeared seconds later, as though not missed.

CHAPTER THIRTY-TWO

Kevin watched Gloria scurry around collecting her belongings, tossing them with a haphazard nonchalance into an oversized suitcase, her husky voice muttering, "Throwing me out like a piece of old furniture."

"You'll be fine. You always land on your feet."

"You know you can't live without me."

"Yes, but I can't live with you. This is the best for both of us."

She whirled around to face him, holding a tissue-thin negligee.

He took the silk from her hand, folded it carefully, and placed it on top of the already-packed clothing. There was something irresistible that drew Kevin to Gloria, and even though they'd been divorced for more than twenty years, she overpowered him with her allure. It just seemed to come naturally for her, she was the waves of a warm ocean. The pull he felt grabbed him in the chest to dive in. He was once again that seven-year-old being led by his mother, the woman who bent his every moment to her needs and wants. He was simply her child until he'd gathered his strength and broken free.

"I will miss you."

"You bet you will."

"Gloria, don't get nasty."

She clicked the lock on one suitcase, opened a second suitcase, and pointed to the empty space. "This is exactly how I feel. Empty." Her voice lowered to a whisper. "I lost my contract."

"I knew that must have been the reason you finally came back to New York."

"They had the nerve to tell me I was too old. Can you imagine?" She slumped on the bed and looked up at Kevin, her eyes sunken. "I'm broke."

"I surmised as much." He sat down on the bed next to her, and placed his arm around her shoulders.

"You don't know what it's like, being a woman and told you're all washed up, that your days of modeling are over, of no longer being photographed. I was on magazine covers over and over again. It's been my life. My career. All these years it's been about my face and my body, and I had to keep it in shape. And it cost me a lot of money to do that."

Kevin felt her shudder.

"I had to keep myself wanted by the agencies. The photographers. That's all I've ever known. I don't have resources like you, with your money passed from generation to generation. I have no one to fall back on. You're the only one who matters in my life. Those managers and agents, they don't give a shit about me as a person. I was just a thing they could throw away, sweep out of the door like smelly day-old garbage, tear into tiny pieces and fling aside."

Eyes overflowing with tears, she crumbled, pressing her head on Kevin's chest. "Can't we work something out? Please don't make me go."

Kevin held the trembling body nestling its way back into his heart. He felt her tears were like a waterfall that would never end. He longed for the woman she once was, their days together, his pride having her hand in his, her warm breath on his cheek. He felt the weight of her hurt deep in his heart. He'd do almost anything to help her. She was his innocent love, and still beautiful in his eyes.

Rocking her gently, he had to remind himself that she was a champion of manipulation, of obtaining her wishes at all cost. He'd fallen for a ruse once too often.

CHAPTER THIRTY-THREE

The phone dangled from Irene's hand. Progress was an uphill battle. At every turn it was as though boulders blocked her road to divorce, trees mired her way, thorns scratched and prodded and tried to dig into her resolve. Stuck in neutral, unable to go forward, it was precisely the way Ashford wanted it, and just for the flick of a moment, she wondered if it all was worth it.

Irene stormed from Julia's small apartment feeling as though her life had been put on hold for far too long. Her attorney's advice was to do nothing and wait it out, saying that Ashford couldn't avoid a separation agreement forever. She had her doubts, knowing that the bastard would like nothing better than to see her struggle.

Speed-walking down the avenue, her heart was going a mad pace, tossing her quandary from right to left; get a job, yes or no; move or not move; buy or rent; multiple issues tumbled topsy-turvy, like wooden building blocks falling any which way in a mayhem of a child's temper tantrum.

Finally reaching 58th Street, one block north of Carnegie Hall, Irene stopped, steadied herself and wiped the moisture from her forehead. Seeking a sense of hope, she counted to ten, and entered the store. Greeting her was the faint smell of lemon oil and a mountain range of pianos; grand pianos, uprights, digital, new and rebuilt, so well restored it was difficult to tell the new from the previously owned.

She wandered around from one make to another, feeling as though she had entered a paradise. Toward the back of the store was an open area arranged as a concert venue, the perfect setting for student recitals. Approaching a black Steinway, her fingers itched. The white ivories winked at her, the black keys stood at the ready. She trailed her fingertips over the ebony finish. It felt like satin. Circling the magnificent beast, she felt its stillness, waiting for her to bring life to the hammers and strings.

The fall board was open. She sat down on the bench before the black beauty, and placed her foot upon the soft pedal. Lifting her hands, she began a simple Chopin, putting breath into the notes and chords. To her ears, the sound was full and the keys had a sensitive touch. Next, her fingers sampled a section of a Beethoven symphony. She sat back, rubbed her fingers together, and lifted her hands well above the keyboard. As though of their own volition, they played a portion of Debussy's Children's Corner Suite.

"Professional?" asked a man in a dark pin-striped suit and tie, his voice filled with gavel.

Startled, Irene simply shook her head. So completely engrossed in the music, she'd lost all sense of her whereabouts.

"Classically trained. That's obvious."

She paused, then stroked the keys with a tender touch and played a combination of pop music and Sinatra melodies. When she was finished and stood behind the bench, the man said, "I'm the owner, Alex Menton. You looking to purchase or rent?"

The floor tilted, as though it was falling away from her. "I'm not certain."

"Why don't you try some of the other makes," he waved his hand in introduction to the vast assortment.

She smiled and took one step back. "I really like this beauty."

"It is a model 'S.'"

"I need to think this over."

"I'm certain we can work with you on price."

She wondered if a purchase like this would mean haggling, like buying a car, or if she could maintain her composure and continue this pretense. "Give me your best price, short and sweet."

The man wrote down some figures and handed the paper to Irene. "Thirty-two thousand is really the best I can do on a purchase. If you need to pay it off in time, I'll have to adjust that. Now, if you decide on a rental, there's the monthly cost plus security."

Weak in the knees, Irene shifted from foot to foot, looked at the paper, and placed it in her purse. "I have to think about this." She smiled graciously, thanked Menton for his time, tapped the baby grand, and walked out onto the street. There, she leaned against the building, her knees giving way. Music was the one thing she still had. If there was anything Irene had ever loved, it was a baby grand piano. Sitting before it felt like a first love's fulfillment. Someday, maybe she'd wrap one up and take it home.

When her heart slowed, and she could breathe normally, she walked at a slow pace down the block, envisioning the piano in an apartment she would eventually call her home. She passed guitars hanging in store windows, violins and trumpets, the sound of a harp floated from an open door.

Watching cars move slowly along the street, impatient drivers honking horns, Irene knew she needed patience above all else. Eventually, if events went her way, there would be a bevy of children to teach. She felt renewed, refreshed, able to tackle whatever obstacles Ashford threw at her.

Down the street, a man in a tattered jacket was playing a saxophone, his eyes half closed as the music soared over the city sounds. On the sidewalk next to the musician's scruffy boots was an empty hat. Irene dug into her purse and dropped a five-dollar bill into the hat, wondering how long she could afford to help others.

CHAPTER THIRTY-FOUR

Though it was close to midnight, the narrow streets of Greenwich Village were thriving like a holiday sale at Macy's. Night brought artists from their studios. An autumn wind whipped down the street, lifting a newspaper off the sidewalk, flattening it against a brick building. A stray dog peed on a fire hydrant. A tall man with a crazy juggler's hat stumbled across the street. The mouth-watering aroma of a kabob sizzling on a grill mingled with the musty smell of old buildings. This part of the city was alive at all hours.

Riley linked her arm through Nick's, drawing them close together. "I have a little goodie for you."

"Yea?"

"It's a surprise. Guess."

"I hate that."

"Are we near the club yet?"

"Two blocks."

She pulled him away from the street light and took something from the pocket of her shorts. "We'll each have one. Something to make the night memorable."

"Uppers?"

"Yup!"

"Where did they come from? Gloria? Her prescription?"

"No! But if I'd known she had a stash—"

"I can't." Nick heaved a deep breath, and turned his face away.

"Come on, Nick, just one to take the edge off."

"I won't, and you shouldn't, either."

"Don't be a dick."

"Think! Think about the days we spent in the sober house, swearing to never again sink. We're each other's support. I won't let you do this!"

She tilted her head to the side, her voice sliding into the picture of a Southern belle. "Oh, don't be like that." Nuzzling his neck, she murmured, "Tonight should be fun. Don't you want to have a good time with me? Remember the time we ran down that path to the beach."

"How could I forget? We were a tangle of arms and legs."

"Hot, Nick. Really hot! A total trip and a half."

"And then? After that?" He let the question dangle for a moment, recalling the nausea, the sweats and tremors, the bottom they had each reached. Promises, so many promises: to Kevin, to Riley, and to himself. He stood frozen in place. His jaw twitched. "You know what happened after. You know what you're heading for. You don't want that. I don't want that."

The wind gusted around Riley's long legs. She stood back, fast in her combat boots, her fist clenched in front of Nick's face. "A little one is all."

Nick grabbed her wrist and forced her hand open to a pile of white pills. "Just throw them away."

Riley's lips pulled into a straight line, and she lifted the open hand as an offering to Nick. "You do it."

"You stole them. You get rid of them." Nick could feel the saliva gather, his determination crack. The snake of desire coiled in his belly.

CHAPTER THIRTY-FIVE

Back in his own bedroom, no longer sleeping in the library, Kevin found he was chasing sleep to no avail. A melody played and replayed in his head. He couldn't shake it. He counted sheep, recited the alphabet backwards, created a multiplication chart picturing a blackboard and chalk. Nothing helped. His thoughts kept circling the empty apartment. No one had greeted him with a hug, or a hello, or a drink in hand.

His home was unnaturally quiet. The entry lights cast shadows, the dining table had not been set, and the kitchen sink remained full of breakfast dishes, but the scent of Gloria's perfume was everywhere, a haunting memory of her presence. He knew that if Gloria was still in the apartment, she would have something amongst her prescriptions that would help him sleep. She'd gone just as he'd demanded, and Nick and Riley had yet to come home.

He flung off the comforter, put on his bathrobe, and made his way to the kitchen. He opened the sub-zero refrigerator and scanned the items without interest. He checked the pantry for some forgotten sweet, backed away and slumped against the counter top. The same solemn melody played over and over in his mind, and his fingertips ran on the granite, as though plucking the strings of his guitar.

As dawn crept to the city, Kevin opened the latch on his guitar case and began the somber melody, a refrain from *Aida*, the words of the aria expressing hope. Kevin played, strumming and plucking the strings, and as morning sun flooded his living room, he improvised on the theme of rescuing the captured princess, changing his classical style to that of cool jazz, composing a piece, smiling at the new sounds and rhythms.

He jotted down the notes on a hastily pulled piece of blank paper, sketched a bit of the music as a reminder of the distinct style he'd rendered, showered, dressed, and walked a brisk pace to his office, humming and improvising on the tune, eager for his work day to end.

Neither the crowds on the street nor the elevator to his offices stopped the notes from playing in his head. Humming to himself, he passed the receptionist, the secretaries, the glass cubicles, and his assistant, and managed the ritual "hellos," the musical notes continuing to soar before his eyes as the sound danced in the air.

Though distracted, Kevin spent the morning dictating a letter to his secretary, held a lengthy meeting with a bank official, and interviewed a real estate broker for an onsite project, yet underlying every thought lay a deep tone of unrest. The music turned dark. Where had Riley and Nick spent the night?

Kevin turned his desk chair toward the window, and like the blades of a windmill spinning in his mind, worry about Nick burst to the forefront. The lines at the corners of his eyes deepened as he recalled the many shrill midnight phone calls. They had come sounding an alarm, breaking into the stupor of deep sleep. He remembered the first call, when Nick was but thirteen, and how his hand shook fumbling for the phone, hoping against hope that it was a crank call. The dark-of-the-night calls escalated and were etched, deeply engraved on his mind as though on a dog tag hung from his neck. He closed his hands into fists, remembering the first of repeated calls.

"Nick's in jail." Gloria's husky voice sounded of defeat.

"What for?"

"Drunk and disorderly."

"Did you speak with him?"

"Just now."

"Can't you keep him out of trouble?"

"That's your job! You're his father."

Kevin swung his chair back toward the desk while guilt washed over him. He phoned Nick, and again heard that the mailbox was full. He shook his head, thinking he could not live his son's life, but hoping that trouble had not found Nick again, that he had not fallen into the well of drugs.

CHAPTER THIRTY-SIX

Fascinated by his hands, the withered flesh and blue veins, Irene watched her attorney riffle through the sheaf of papers, his head of snow white hair bobbing each time he turned to the next page, and the next, and the next. Shifting in the leather chair, her foot jiggled up and down. Time was rolling. She tore her focus from the attorney to the paneled walls, to the polished wood book cases, to the window, where the puffy clouds of early afternoon had turned deep grey. Rain was in the forecast. A storm was brewing.

Irene's funds were being swallowed, her patience gobbled with each turning page, until finally the attorney closed the file and placed his hands flat on top. As though having a second thought, he re-opened the file and pulled out one paper, his chin ducking into his neck. "You are certain you never signed this?"

She looked at the elderly attorney, his lips drawn into a fine line. She saw doubt in his eyes. It wasn't compassion she was after. Irene wanted acknowledgment of the truth. "That so-called pre-nuptial paper, I never signed that agreement. I swear that signature is not mine. Ashford is not beneath anything to get what he wants, and that's to destroy me, leave me penniless and homeless. Then he'll be satisfied."

She crossed her arms in front of herself. "I told you before, I'd never seen that agreement until I dug the papers from Ashford's desk. You believe me, don't you? This is one of Ashford's schemes. It was buried in the pile of papers I copied from Ashford's desk drawer. We've been over this before. Can't we get on with a separation agreement? Something?"

"Mrs. Aubrey, unfortunately, there has been no response from Mr. Aubrey."

"You mean in all this time, I'm exactly where I started?"

"Only that now we are certain if you wish to continue, this will go to court. And I'm sorry to say, that will take a good deal of time."

Irene jumped up and swallowed the rising bile. "This is like a bad novel. It's his scheme to make me—"

"Please, sit down."

"But I…"

"I understand your frustration."

"You have no idea." She flung herself back onto the chair, and buried her face in her hands. "I'm at my wits' end. I'm still sleeping on my friend's couch, like a high school kid running away from home." She looked up at the still figure of her attorney. "I can't do this anymore."

"Mrs. Aubrey. If you choose to sue for divorce, you may have to face a divorce trial."

"Oh my God, airing all our dirty linen in public."

"No, no, Mrs. Aubrey. Going to court is nothing like that. It's a legal method by which contracts are broken or changed. There is a determined process in a contested divorce. You understand, the state has the right to ascertain whether your marriage can be dissolved."

"What?" Irene flinched, fell against the back of the chair, her eyes wild as though a trapped raccoon.

"Marriage is a legally binding contract that you signed on your wedding day."

Irene closed her eyes, hoping this nightmare would disappear. Rubbing her temples with her forefingers, she wondered, and not for the first time, if this attorney was in her corner. Money was being spent with nothing to show for the hours. "Just get it done. I don't care which way."

"This all takes time."

"What kind of time?"

"When the husband is devious and cunning, or like Mr. Aubrey, makes himself unavailable, I've known a divorce to take upwards of five years. Going to trial can be costly. Are you prepared for this?"

Irene turned her head away. The very idea of litigation was terrifying. For a split second, she thought of returning to Ashford. With that horrifying thought, her blood turned to ice and drained from her face. Lightheaded, she blinked to clear her vision. "I can't afford to go on and on like this. I don't have an endless pit of monies. Ashford can keep this going for as long as it takes for me to give up."

Leaning on the desk for support, the attorney rose from his chair and stumbled around the desk. "Maybe you should think about your own peace of mind, and move on with your life."

Bolting upright from her chair, she stood with defiance on her shoulders. "Maybe I should."

She raced down the three flights of stairs, barely breathing. She did not want to take the elevator and risk someone, anyone, seeing her in this current state of disarray, or see the hysteria that danced, looming over her every muscle and tendon. Her future was bleak. She stood on the landing between floors, leaned against the concrete wall, and managed to bring herself to a state of reality. Ashford would do anything he could to put her under, but she would survive.

She called his cell, regretting it the moment he answered.

"Changed your mind yet?"

"No."

"I wondered for a moment how you were surviving. You should be here. I'm sitting on top of the world, having an elegant lunch looking out over the city. Even though the skyline is in the clouds, the view never ceases to amaze."

"Please, Ashford. We shouldn't end up court."

"Listen to me carefully: I will not allow a divorce to smirch my good name. When your foolishness is over and forgotten, you'll see that you belong home as my adoring wife."

"Please, Ashford, I'm not asking much. Be fair. Ashford, please, let go of me."

"Trust me, Irene, I will eat you up alive."

CHAPTER THIRTY-SEVEN

Fidgeting at lunch in a tiny French restaurant, Kevin quenched his thirst with a glass of chilled chardonnay, his appetite appeased with a cup of onion soup along with a mushroom-crab-asparagus tart. He listened with half an ear to his assistant list the complaints from a condominium association and all the day-to-day details of administering management services.

His attention flickered from his cell phone to the elderly group seated at the next table, to the paintings on the wall, and back across the table to Walter, his assistant. Forearms on the white table cloth, Kevin leaned forward. "In the three years you've been with the company, I know nothing about your life."

"That shouldn't be an issue, as long as I do my job to your satisfaction." Walter flashed his smile, folded and placed his napkin on the table.

"Oh, no, don't think for one moment that you've disappointed me. Not in the least. I was just curious. I don't even know if you're married, or single, or have a child."

"Married, divorced, and have a child," he shrugged his broad shoulders. "And that about sums up my life."

"That can't be all."

"Okay. Born in Staten Island,. and lived in Manhattan all my life."

"That's not telling me much. How about hobbies?"

"No, but I play a bit of golf now and then."

"Children?"

A long moment passed, then Kevin raised his eyebrows and asked, "Do you have a son or daughter?"

"A son. He's about the age of your boy, Nick."

Kevin smoothed his fingertips over his cell phone. His mind wandered, and stuck on the thought that perhaps Nick and Riley were at Gloria's apartment. "Excuse me, a moment." Kevin pushed the auto-dial, listened for the recording and left a message.

Turning his attention back across the table, Kevin said, "Sorry about that. You were telling me something about your son. What's his name?"

Walter said something inaudible.

"I'm sorry, what did you say."

"Nothing important." Walter's focus shifted, and he looked over Kevin's shoulder. "He's gay."

"Who?"

"My son, Wesley. He's gay." He pinched his lips and made a deep sound. "When he told me, I didn't handle it well."

"We all have faults." Kevin flattened his hand on the table, and nodded toward Walter, thinking this man was someone he saw on a daily basis and just now noticed the pain in his eyes. Where was his insight? Did pain show in his own eyes?

"I've tried over and over again to apologize. He won't speak to me."

"We're all human. None of us are perfect."

"I've tried. You have no idea how hard I tried." He shook his head, took his napkin and dabbed at the tip of his nose. "It's like I'm dead to him."

"Don't give up trying. One day he may understand, accept your apology and reach out to you."

"I just hope it's not too late."

The words repeated in Kevin's mind. He, too, hoped it was not too late.

A few moments of silence as each of the men thought of his own missteps. The waiter cleared the dishes and served them double espressos and portions of chocolate mousse topped with whipped cream. Kevin picked up his spoon and broke into the dessert, took a small sample, then sipped from the tiny cup.

As though the prior conversation was tucked away, Kevin signaled for the check and asked, "What's left on the list?"

The assistant cleared his throat, returning to business as though from some foreign place. "Last on the long list, they want you to attend the next board meeting."

"That's not going to happen."

"All they really want is for you to fire the concierge."

"Again? That building has had more staff changes than any other. What's the problem?"

"They're not happy with his attitude."

Kevin impatiently signaled the waiter a second time for the check. "Who's the board president?"

"I'll have to check on that, but I think his name is Ashford Aubrey."

CHAPTER THIRTY-EIGHT

The rain was coming down in torrents when Irene paid the cab driver, thinking perhaps that was her last taxi ride. Life was all a matter of priorities. Buses and subways and her own two feet would get her where she had to go from now on. Within seconds, she was soaked. The rain penetrated her wool jacket, letting water trickle down her back and seeped onto her silk sweater. Her hair had come undone, dripped around her ears and neck, and wet locks slapped at her face when she rounded the corner.

Hurrying to Julia's apartment, she stepped off the curb into a huge puddle, stumbled, and twisted her ankle. A full blast of cold wind ripped right into her ribs. She lifted her face to the downpour as if to shout, "What next?"

In Julia's apartment, she sank like a wet sack onto the couch and curled as a snail, holding onto herself, burying her face in the pillows. It had been another day without progress. She hadn't meant to be flippant with her attorney. Her funds were dwindling. Hour upon hour had been wasted in waiting.

Curling tighter, her fingers gripped her shoulders. Chilled and shivering, she flinched, her leg twitched, her jaw tightened. Whimpering, her sobs—which began as a snivel—suddenly wrenched from her core a cry of anguish. Wasn't this what she wanted? Away from living with Ashford, to answer for herself, not be a pawn to his abusive behavior. She was on her own.

She went into the bathroom, pulled a towel from the hook, brushed her hair out straight, pulled off her clothing, washed the makeup from her face, and peered in the mirror. Shriveling before the reflection, she saw a beaten woman, thin and scared. Looking in the full-length mirror, she judged the image, and said aloud, "That woman is not me."

Her face set with determination, Irene went to the closet, grabbed dry clothing from her suitcase, dressed, borrowed a raincoat and umbrella from Julia, and went out to meet the storm, resolute to turn over a new page in her story. No longer would she be cowed by the futility of waiting for her life to begin. Moving ahead would be her mantra, with gratitude at the beginning of each new day.

The rain had slacked off to a light drizzle. The afternoon was drawing to a close, night was falling along with the temperature. Irene flung the cashmere silk scarf loosely around her neck. Her first stop was the drug store. where she bought back her gold wedding band for the price of a box of band aids. Then she preceded east toward Lincoln Center.

At the box office, Irene purchased one of the last seats available for the evening's performance of *Don Giovanni*, the role of Donna Ana to be sung by Renee Fleming. Seated in the upper gallery on the edge of her seat, she applauded as the curtain rose. The stage appeared as a doll house, the characters so tiny Irene could hardly distinguish one from another, but their voices rang true to her last seat in the balcony, even though the final scene—when the earth opened and Don Giovanni is pulled into Hell—was hardly visible. How vastly different the stage looked to Irene seated in the upper balcony, rather than the prime seats of Ashford's subscription.

Outside, the rain had stopped. Limousines streamed away from the curb, taxis jockeyed for position, crowds waited to cross the street, and Irene walked back toward Julia's apartment, musing on the finale scene. A smile crossed her face, thinking that Giovanni got his comeuppance, exactly what he deserved. She crossed the avenue, reviewing in her mind the duplicity and violence of Mozart's plot. In the opera, resentment turned to pity, and Irene wondered if her bitterness toward Ashford would eventually turn.

So focused she almost tripped over a woman who was plastered against the brick building. The woman half sat, half lay on her side. Next to her was a pile of torn and bulging plastic garbage bags. She was barefoot, and wore a filthy torn shirt. Scabs ran up her bare legs, and her grey hair lay flat on her scalp. Under the street lamp, Irene saw dark blue circles under the woman's eyes, eyes that were deep as though she'd seen too much of life.

Irene pulled the coat tight around herself, gripped the umbrella, and walked away a few steps before turning back. Removing the expensive scarf from her neck, she placed it gently over the woman's torso, and put a five-dollar bill in the woman's hand.

CHAPTER THIRTY-NINE

Riley, sprawled on the single bed, moaned, rolled onto her side, and retched onto a towel set on the worn carpet.

Nick dabbed at her mouth with a wet washcloth, and wiped the vomit from her chin. "Learned your lesson?" He picked up the dirty towel and dumped it in the bathtub along with the others, took a clean washcloth from the rack, and wet it with cold water. He closed the bathroom door as though the odious smell would stay there and not permeate the hotel room any further than it already had.

Nick leaned an arm across Riley and placed the cloth over her eyes. "Sleep?"

"No." She flung the cloth off, pushed his arm, and sat bent over next to him, her hands over her ears as though blocking a deafening trumpet, the wet cloth on the floor. Rubbing at her throat as though it was sore, she said in a croaking voice, "What the hell."

He got up and walked across the narrow room. "You don't even know what that stuff was. You threw all those pills down your throat."

"I don't remember."

"Was that to spite me?"

"Stop talking."

"You don't remember, huh? The club?" Dancing? Falling all over yourself?"

She shook her head.

"You don't remember that guy with the tattooed arms? You don't remember going with him to the back? Taking whatever the hell he gave you, snuggling up to him until pulled you away?" He pressed his forehead on the streaked wall. "God, Riley!"

Again, she raised her shoulders and gestured ignorance. It was then she noticed the bruises on her thin arms, smudges of black and blue just beginning to turn yellow. Stumbling to the bathroom, she flung open the door and gagged a dry heave into the sink, then sank to the tile floor, gripped the edge of the white porcelain sink, and pulled herself upright, the sink wobbling from its base. The mirror she faced reflected scratches on her neck, and dried blood on her nostrils.

She stripped out of the stained skimpy top, torn shorts and lace thong, pulled aside the shower curtain, and turned the faucet on full. The water pipe shuddered behind the broken tile until delivered a mere trickle of warm, orange-tinted water. Riley climbed into the tub, stood under the dripping shower head, pushing away the dirty towels with her feet, her hands plastered against the prefabricated wall as though trying to remember her lost hours. "Bloody hell. This place is a shit hole."

Nick leaned against the door frame. "I couldn't very well take you home in your condition. If Kevin saw us, it would be all over."

"Where did you take me? Some flea bag motel?"

"God, Riley, you should be grateful I didn't leave you with that creep."

She flung aside the curtain, pulling it off its hooks. "Grateful? Look at my arms. My neck. How can I model looking like this?"

"You should have thought about that before gobbling all those pills."

"I remember now, you grabbed me and dragged me away and into the street. Look! Look! Take a good look at what you've done!"

"You did it all to yourself."

Nick turned away, slammed the door to the bathroom closed, and sank on the thin mattress, his head held in his hands. His mouth was dry, and there was a gnawing in the pit of his stomach. The craving was back. There again was the familiar wave crushing him, pushing the breath from his will. He banged his forehead with the heel of his hand to stop the waves crashing over him. He was a drowning man. He gulped oxygen. One little pill would bring release from the storm. A mere pill, and he could float above the rising waters, drift above the thrashing waves.

Out of the room as though chased by a demon, Nick raced out onto the street. Sweat broke out on his forehead as he ran farther south to his old haunts, to people he knew and to places he could get what he needed, paying no attention to the rain soaking through his jacket, streaming down his forehead. He crossed against traffic, ran between cars, didn't care about anything but a fix. There, amongst cabs jockeying for position, trucks blocking the intersection, blaring horns, Nick was hit from behind by a messenger riding a bicycle.

His feet flew out from under him, one loafer hitting the windshield of a delivery truck, his left foot pinned under the tire of a slow-moving van.

CHAPTER FORTY

Kevin stayed at the office a bit longer, watching the dark sky, listening to the incessant rain which continued to beat on the city, flooding drains and slowing traffic. He often liked to take a brisk walk to stretch his legs after a long day of desk work. On this day, the rains had thwarted his desire, and it had been necessary to zigzag the crowded streets and puddles to reach his destination, the monthly Board of Directors meeting.

He thought of this condominium building as the best of the best, the crown jewel of his management company. Kevin's company had administered this site for six years, and too often his employees had been questioned and criticized by the president of the board. Against his better judgment, Kevin had agreed that after the general meeting an issue involving one of the doormen would be discussed.

He entered the back of the roof-top multi-purpose room. His eyes roamed over the large room, filled to capacity with owners and tenants. The scent of expensive perfume mingled with that of wet clothing. A line of speakers waited their turn at the microphone. Kevin had no hope that this meeting would soon draw to a close. He plunked his umbrella in the stand amongst the others. Shoes oozing water onto the plush carpet, he took a seat toward the back of the room.

The President of the Board, Ashford Aubrey, was dressed impeccably in a dark blue pin-striped suit, button-down shirt, and dark blue tie, knotted tight around his neck. He looked unfazed by the onslaught of complaints regarding new wallpaper, worn carpeting, slow elevators, but the need for an assessment brought forth loud groans and objections. He addressed each speaker with razor sharp brevity, and cut short their remarks by slamming down his gavel.

Kevin watched Ashford in action, belittling the women and intimidating the men, abusing power to stomp on anyone in his way. He looked familiar, but Kevin was unable to place him. The man was a bully, probably had been all his life. Kevin fingered the scar above his eye, remembering the bullies in grade school. He'd stood up to them then, and the scar was a constant reminder of standing his ground. No one would intimidate him. Kevin made a note to check the building's annual financial statement and recent minutes.

When the meeting was closed, Ashford strode directly toward the back of the room. Standing, Kevin extended his hand and while shaking Ashford's, he suddenly recognized him from the performance of *Aida*. Odd, he thought, that in a city of eight million, threads of Irene kept popping up.

"Quite a large turnout."

"I'm used to it. Everyone who is anyone thinks they have a bright idea. They never do. Stupid people. A big waste of my time."

"The owners take pride in their building and want to—"

"They had nothing of importance to say."

"Actually, are you aware that I own several apartments in this very building?"

"A good investment."

"The Board of Directors of a condominium has a responsibility to listen to everyone and act on their behalf."

"You, Mr. Brooks, as a condo owner and president of the management company, create a conflict of interest. In accordance with our bylaws, an owner cannot be employed in any capacity."

"You'll have to read the amendment issued six years ago, when the board hired my firm. My contract resolves that issue."

"Contracts can be broken."

The men stood like two bucks with their antlers entangled, neither losing nor gaining control. Kevin wondered how long it would take for Ashford to flinch, and was prepared to stay all night if that was the case.

Finally, Ashford took a step forward, toe to toe, his breath hot on Kevin's face, smelled of scotch.

"You will do as I say and fire that Russian doorman."

"Is that the only reason you have demanded I come here?"

"Reason enough."

"I imagine it is because of *you* this building has endured more turnovers of staff than any other."

"Quite rightly. I only tolerate the very best."

As though a bell was about to ring for round one, Kevin raised his chin. "You're quite flippant with people's livelihoods."

"Your staff is here to serve."

"Beyond requests, you have no authority." Kevin collected his umbrella and dug the point into the thick carpet. "I will not fire the doorman."

"You risk losing the management of this building."

"Anything further, speak to my assistant. You and I are finished."

"Don't be so sure!"

CHAPTER FORTY-ONE

Outside of the piano store, Irene reviewed all the possible objections that she was about to confront. Taking a deep breath, she set her back straight, her head high, pushed open the front doors, and strode directly to the owner while extending her hand. "Hi. Remember me? Mrs. Aubrey." She ran her thumb against the gold wedding band.

"Yes. Yes, I thought you might be back."

"Yes, and here I am." Her eyes glided around the store, noting that all the instruments were exactly where they had been last time. Leaning against the nearby piano, her fingertips ran over the ebony wood lid, thinking sales must be stagnant in this business. Feeling a tingle of possibility, her lips lifted in a smile. "I see my favorite is right where I left it."

"She is right here, just waiting for you."

"Are all pianos referred to as 'she'?"

"Only some." His laugh sounded more like a snort.

Irene dug deep into her pocketbook and withdrew a folded piece of paper. "I have an idea that will prove to be good for both of us."

Again she heard that snort as he shook his head. The owner, Mr. Menton, shifted his weight, and his glance fell under drooping eyelids. "I gave you our best price last time you were here."

"Oh that has nothing to do with what I am here to suggest. That is, my husband and I. We have been talking a great deal about the potential here. This space is lying dormant. So many possibilities. I'm so sorry my husband couldn't be with me today.

"Sorry, Mrs. Ah, Mrs.?"

"Aubrey."

"Sorry, but do I know your husband?"

"Of course you do. Ashford Aubrey. He bought a wonderful grand piano from you not ten years ago."

His eyes focused on the far corner of the room as he straightened his jacket and cleared his throat. "Yes. Yes. Now I think I remember him. Drove a hard bargain, if I recall correctly."

She noted the fleck of interest in the man's posture once her husband's name was mentioned.

"Mrs. Aubrey, how can I help you?"

"I have this great idea. It's a bold and innovative plan that will bring new customers to your store, as well as provide students from the group home an opportunity to play the piano." She raised her hand, palm forward. "And, before you say anything, hear me out."

Irene unfolded the paper. "This is a schedule of concerts to be held once a month here in this wonderful store. It's the perfect setting. What better place than here to have a concert for the community?"

"We can't do that."

"Before you say no, just listen." Irene moved away from the owner and glided toward the area she envisioned set for student recitals and the Sunday concerts. Standing in the middle of the space, she could almost hear Julia's flute and Kevin's guitar, and she herself would play the piano, to the applause of a devoted audience.

She felt as though she was a mountain climber reaching for the peak. A broad smile exploded over Irene's face, and the tingle of possibilities raised her shoulders. She'd never been so bold, had never used Ashford's name without his approval, and had never told an outright lie with not a shred of guilt.

"Each month will bring a performance by musicians of the highest quality, for which you will not be billed a single penny. What you will do in exchange, however, is allow me to teach youngsters from nearby one hour each day at the close of the school day. I'll be in touch with the youth service provider on 31st Street, and they will select the children. What a joy this will be. Think not only of the fabulous publicity this will bring, but of the good you will be doing."

The owner tilted his head as though he too was hearing a concert. He licked his bottom lip.

"And how much should the admission be?"

Realizing the man was not hearing the strings of a violin, or the strumming of a guitar, but the sound of money, Irene could see figures adding up in his head.

"Oh no, that's not at all the point. The concerts are to be free to the community. To everyone who wants to attend. We're handing this to people who love music, but have never even thought of stepping into this store."

"I don't know about all this. People milling around. Insurance. I see too many problems."

"You can't buy this kind of publicity. It will be outstanding. Newspapers will come. They'll want to interview you and take photographs. Maybe even the mayor will come. And then," she raised a finger, "musicians, amateurs and pros from the neighborhood who wish to perform with the professionals, can join. Oh, you simply cannot say no to this awesome opportunity."

"Mrs. Aubrey, this is a lot for me to think about: concerts, lessons, I really don't know how this will—"

"Let's give it a try. Just a trial to see how it goes."

Hands deep in his trouser pockets, the owner shook his head. "I don't know about this."

"I'll handle everything. You won't have to do a thing."

"I have to think about—"

"This will be a great success."

He moved toward the outside door, and shook Irene's hand, glancing up at the ceiling. "I have to think it over."

"It'll be the talk of the town."

Once on the sidewalk, Irene could hardly breathe. Her ideas had flowed like a running river. Words had just come, one after another. She'd never been bold. Shrank from confrontation. Called worthless. Her eyes now twinkled as happy tears flowed unhindered down her smiling face.

With long strides and light steps, she walked north past the shops, delighted with herself. She swung her pocketbook back and forth. Like a child, she crossed her fingers, hoping her idea would come to fruition and help those less fortunate.

CHAPTER FORTY-TWO

Kevin, holding a hot cup of black coffee to his lips, heard an odd sound. He cocked his head, listening. His forehead wrinkled. At a second thump, he moved from the kitchen toward the foyer, then raced forward at the sight of Nick swinging a pair of crutches, his left foot heavily bandaged.

"Oh my God, what happened to you?"

"Got run over by a fuckin' truck."

"You what?" Kevin grabbed around Nick's shoulders and helped him to the living room. Nick sank into the couch, the crutches flung to the carpet, and Kevin sat to face him, precariously seated on the edge of the coffee table.

"Tell me what happened? And where's Riley? And where have you two been?"

"One question at a time, please. My head is splitting."

"Tell me what happened."

Nick took a wrinkled pack of cigarettes from his pocket, shook one out and put it to his lips.

"We don't smoke in this house."

"Oh, for God's sake."

"I'll get you an aspirin for your headache. But first, tell me."

"My foot got run over by a truck."

"How on Earth could something like that happen?"

"I got shoved off the curb. By a stupid ass delivery bike."

Kevin's glance shifted to the ceiling. "Is this another one of your stories? Just try for the truth, Nick, I promise I'll listen."

"That'll be new, for a change."

"Just tell me the truth. No more tall tales."

"You always jump to conclusions and think the worst of me."

Kevin got up, picked up the crutches, and leaned them against the back of the couch. He felt that once again, he and his son danced the same scenario. Walking over to the window, Kevin couldn't help but remember the stories he'd listened to over the years, the blame of mishaps never Nick's fault: the burglary, the drugs, jail time served, hooked, rehab, and then rehab again. The failure Kevin felt was in his guts drawing blood from his head. He felt as though time was dormant, that nothing changes. He'd been an absent father, the role model played by Gloria's frequent lovers. It was as though the divorce had been a rock hurled into the center of a pond and the repercussions were evident in the endless ripples and the kid never had a chance. Maybe the usual script would end here and now.

Kevin turned back, picked up a pillow, and placed it behind Nick's head. "Did you get something for pain?"

"I wouldn't take anything."

Kevin cocked his head. "No? You didn't?"

Nick looked up at Kevin towering over him, and spoke as though wrenching the words from an unfathomable depth. "The emergency room offered something for pain, but I didn't want to take it. I was afraid it would start me on drugs again."

"You refused it?"

"It would have been so easy to take, but I knew if I started, I'd never be able to stop again."

Kevin let go a long breath, sat down, and ruffled Nick's hair. "I'm proud of you."

"Yeah." His fists pressed on his thighs, he nodded, "Yeah, I'm clean."

"I know this is tough."

"It's worse."

"Like I've read. They all say, just take it day by day. But aspirin should be fine to take." Kevin checked his watch, got up from the couch, went into the kitchen, and came back with two aspirin on a paper napkin and a glass of water. He placed them on the table in front of Nick. "I have to get to the office. Do you need anything before I go?"

"Nah. I'm fine."

"Call my cell if you need me." He went into his library to pick up his leather attaché case, pleased that Nick had passed a significant hurdle. Perhaps his girlfriend had led him on a clean path, been a good influence. He went back into the living room. "Where's Riley."

"Dunno."

"Wasn't she with you?"

Nick closed his eyes in a grimace, then buried his head in his arms as though sheltering himself. If it hadn't been for his injured foot, he might have curled up in a fetal position and escaped back to Gloria's arms. His voice was weak and thin when he finally said, "She's strung out."

Kevin shook Nick's shoulder. "Look at me! Is she all right?"

With a shudder, his voice wavered. "I don't know."

CHAPTER FORTY-THREE

Irene went directly to the bank, where she withdrew just enough cash for the week's expenses, then proceeded to the vault, where she counted the remaining piles of one-hundred-dollar bills. She closed and locked the vault, walked up the marble staircase to the vast lobby, and pushed through the revolving glass door. Outside, her breath was caught in the chill of a sudden drop in the temperature. Zipping up her down jacket, she walked with a clear sense of security. By her calculations, between the two bank accounts and the cash, if she was cautious, there was enough money to see her through the next six months without undue worry.

Uptown at 76th Street, she entered the café to meet Julia for a light dinner before rehearsal. The walls were adorned with vintage posters. She again admired the Grauer print of black and red called "le secret." She liked the use of just those few colors to indicate a deeply held secret. The poster seemed to talk to Irene, as though it knew her most tightly held secret. Her lips tightened. Everyone has secrets.

The dark paneling and low ceiling held the smell of mouth-watering steaks, reminiscent of her uncle's bar. Behind the heavy wood bar, glass shelves held bottles of top line liquors and spirits, though Irene knew that more times than not, the cheaper house liquors were poured.

Early dinner drew a few diners sitting at scattered tables. The sudden laughter of a middle-aged couple caught Irene's attention. They were sitting, pitched forward toward each other, holding hands across the small café table. Their delight was contagious, drawing a smile across Irene's face. At the same time, she was overcome with a sense of envy.

Irene chose to sit near the piano alcove just as Julia pushed opened the door and entered along with a gust of cold air. She carried the flute case clasped tight to her chest, and sat down on the empty chair across from Irene. "Whew. It's freezing already, and it's not even December."

With a tilt of her head, Irene indicated the couple gazing intently into each other's eyes. "Don't they look happy?"

"Who?"

"Them. The lovebirds over there. Have you ever had that?"

"What?" Julia struggled out of her overcoat, flung it on an empty chair, and signaled the waiter.

"That feeling of being with someone who knows you and loves you and cares what you care about? Seeing them fills me up and then empties me out, like a dried-up piece of fruit waiting to be tossed aside."

"It's too cold for fruit salad."

Irene leaned forward. "You didn't hear a word I said."

"If it's a complaint or a worry, I'm not interested."

"God, Julia. What's gotten into you. What's the matter?"

"What's the matter with you? You take yourself so seriously. Always have."

Irene sat up straighter in her chair. "Are you angry with me? Did I do something?"

"Don't mind me. I always get this way around the holidays."

The waiter approached with pencil and pad at the ready. "Are you ladies ready to order?"

Julia nodded her head. "I always order the same thing, every time I'm here: hamburger medium well on a bun, with French fries very well done. And I'll have a glass of house pinot grigio."

"Same for me, but no fries. I'll have a wedge of lettuce and tomatoes instead. And yes, the wine, absolutely."

After the waiter left, Irene's attention was again drawn to the lovebirds. "Aren't they irresistible?"

"You're staring at them."

"Do you think they're married?"

Julia looked toward them. "Not likely."

The couple got up from the table, and the man helped the woman with the buttons on her coat. He drew her close, and then they left the café, the cold night air sweeping along the wide planks of the wooden floor.

Julia shifted her weight on the chair as the wine was delivered. "I shouldn't have ordered the fries. It's like a reflex whenever I'm in here. Same old, same old. They say it only takes twenty-one days to break a habit. I just can't decide which to break: the wine or the fries."

"You can always push the fries aside."

"We could trade plates. I'll eat your rabbit food, and you have my delicious potatoes."

"Instead of the wine, you can always have club soda with a big piece of lime or lemon."

"You think?"

"You can do it if you really want to lose those extra pounds."

Julia looked straight at Irene, her eyes narrowed. "Have you forgotten who I am? I love my fries and wine." She grasped the glass of wine and took a huge gulp. "Oh my God, I'm sorry. I've completely lost control of myself."

Irene saw worry lines deepen on Julia's forehead. "Is something wrong? You look so worried. Tell me."

"I don't know how to tell you." With a heave of breath, she said, "My sister is coming for Thanksgiving."

"That's wonderful."

"She always comes at turkey time, disrupting my entire life. Telling me what to do and what not to do."

Slowly, the meaning of this news dawned on Irene. Her high cheeks softened. She didn't feel unmoored. Most surprising, it was not what she would have expected at the loss of housing. Instead, a sense of renewed liberation spread. What she felt was relief.

Her thoughts carried her to a place she could call her own, some place with a piano. She'd get one, even one that had been neglected, with ivories turned yellow, beaten wood and sticky keys. She would get it tuned properly, have the tension readjusted, replace some of the strings if necessary. She'd bring it back to life.

Julia drank the last of her wine with a gulp. She took her napkin and rubbed a spot on the table, interrupting the silence that had fallen between them. "She'd never forgive me if I told her not to come."

"How great, the two of you spending time together. Of course, I'll move out in plenty of time."

"We don't get along that well, and I hate that I'm tossing you out with no place to go."

"Julia," her voice low as though telling a child something they should know, "I can always go to a hotel." Then she reached across the table, and with a soft touch, placed her palm on Julia's arm. "Please, I'm grateful. I don't mean just for your hospitality, but for your friendship. You've helped me in more ways than I can count. I owe you lots. Tomorrow I'll go look for a place."

"Sure you're ready for a reality check? Rents are sky high. You know, we can always buy a cot and move it into—"

"Don't be ridiculous. I'll either rent or maybe purchase a condo. Wanna go hunting with me? Let's make it fun."

The waiter arrived, placing their plates before them. Julia glanced down at the fries, and then looked across the table and pushed her plate forward. "Change with me?"

Irene took Julia's dinner, moved the fries to the side, doused her burger with ketchup, and nibbled at the edges while Julia wolfed down her hamburger, juices running onto her sweater. "I shouldn't eat so much before rehearsal."

"Will you and Kevin play that tango again?"

"He has a new piece he wants us to try. I'm anxious to hear it. He said it just came to him one night when he couldn't sleep. He wrote it for the three of us. It's based on a theme from *Aida*."

CHAPTER FORTY-FOUR

Pacing back and forth in front of the photographer, Gloria's spike heels ticked the stone floor in rapid fire. Holding the cell tight against her ear, she plastered a smile across her face, and pressed the automatic phone number for Nick.

"Nick will know where she is. They're always together. I can't imagine what has happened. This is not like her in the least."

"I won't wait much longer."

The muscles of Gloria's face quivered. A vein on her forehead twitched. She heard Nick's voice message box was full. She shouted into the recording, "Nick, god-damn-it, answer the phone."

The camera man tapped meaningfully on his wristwatch. "This is the first and last time you'll find me waiting. Who does she think she is? I'm out of here." He unscrewed a lens from one camera, covered it with a felt wrapper, and put it aside. "As far as I am concerned, her career is over."

Turning away from the photographer, Gloria punched in the automatic number for Kevin's cell, and as soon as he answered, she blurted, "Where're Nick and Riley?"

"And hello to you, too," he answered.

"Riley hasn't shown up for her shoot, and I need her now."

"You sound rattled."

"Where are they?"

"Nick's at my apartment with a—"

"Riley? She's there?"

"No, and I—"

"Where is she?"

"She's not with Nick, and he doesn't know where she is. If you'd listen to me for one second, you—"

"After all I've done for that girl, she's left me here with her contract being ripped to shreds, and my reputation along with it. I have to get her here in the next five minutes or she'll have to deal with this on her own. I give up, on both of them."

"Gloria. Listen to me."

"I need her right now. Tell him to get her to me."

"That's not going to happen."

"And why the hell not? Doesn't Nick know where she is?"

"The simple answer is 'no'."

"What am I supposed to do now? Kevin, think of something. I went out on a limb for her! It's my reputation. Think of the consequences for me. I'm struggling to keep this together. Help me out here."

"Gloria, stop thinking about yourself and calm down. I need to tell you something." He paused. "Nick had a bit of an accident, but he's okay."

"Accident? What? I can't believe this. You have him under your roof for one month and he has an accident. He never had an accident when he was in my home. Where is he? What have you done to him?"

Kevin simply shook his head with the thought that Gloria will always be Gloria. "He's resting in the living room."

"Stay right there. I'm coming. Just you wait right there."

"I'm not at home. I'm at my office."

"You left my son alone?"

With a curl of her lip, Gloria snapped the phone, ending the call. She charged from the photographer's studio, flagged a cab to Kevin's building, and flew up the elevator to the apartment. Crossing the entry, Gloria marched down the hall directly into the living room and flung her cashmere coat onto a side chair.

Nick lay on the couch. His jaw drooped with saliva gathering at the corners of his lips. He jerked awake as though from a nightmare, and saw Gloria standing over him.

"Crutches? Nick, you're on crutches! Why didn't you call me?" She bent down, shook him by the shoulders. "You could have been killed. What accident? What would I have done if you'd been killed!" She placed her hand across him forehead.

At the cool touch of her palm, he flinched back slightly. His emerald eyes sought Gloria's. "Okay. Okay. Just my foot."

"How did this happen?"

"Just happened."

"Tell me. Tell me the truth. Were you on something?"

"Is that the first thing you want to ask me? How about, how're you feeling. Are you in pain?"

Gloria nodded, backed away. "You're right. Does it hurt?"

"Not right now."

"That's good. Where's Riley? She put me in an unbearable position. Now, where is she? Hiding from my wrath?"

His voice dropped to a lower volume. "Dunno."

"She's finished. Great career never really started."

Gloria threw off her high heels, flopped back on the armchair, and let out a huff. "I could wring her neck. I'm exhausted."

Nick lay his head back down on the pillow.

"Tell me, damn it, why she didn't show up for me. Has she been hurt?"

"No." Nick, a sour taste in his mouth, took the crumpled pack of cigarettes from his back pocket. He fumbled for his lighter, remembering that on the coffee table in Gloria's home, a crystal lighter stood gleaming, a gift from one of her past lovers.

"You know Kevin won't allow you to smoke in here. How did you break your foot?"

"It's not broken. It got crushed under a car."

"How on Earth…?"

"Shit happens."

"And you came here."

"Yup."

"Straight? Were you on something?"

"For the third time, no. I didn't take anything. Not even for the pain. Nothing. I thought both you and Kevin would be proud of me. Instead, you both attack me, bombard me with questions and assume I'd been high. You should know, everyone around me was doing everything. It would have been so easy to join in and just let go for a while. My God, Gloria, the temptation was everywhere. And I stood solid."

Nick grimaced. Rubbing his knees as though in physical pain, he shook his head and ducked his chin to his chest. "I know I have a bad history and have told some tall tales. But, now, for the first time, I'm telling you the absolute truth." He squeezed his lips together. "I'm proud of myself."

"I didn't mean to accuse you."

"I didn't mean to jump on you."

Gloria went over to the couch and sat down next to Nick. Placing her palm on his shoulder, her emerald eyes narrowing, she said, "It hurts me to see you in pain."

"It'll heal." Nick cast his eyes away from Gloria, reached for the crutches, and managed to pull them close.

"Why isn't Riley here to help you?"

"I don't know where Riley is."

"What do you mean, you don't know."

"Exactly what I said. I don't know where Riley is."

"You're not holding anything back from me. I'm you mother, for God's sake. Are you sure you don't know?"

"I'm not sure of anything. All I know is that right now I'm straight. My fucking foot hurts, but I'm not on anything, not even a god damn cigarette." His voice rose. "I'm not on drugs. You have no idea how tough this is. But I'll say it again so maybe this time you'll hear it."

He stood with the support of the crutches pressed under his armpits. "I'm trying not to go back into drugs. It's tough for me. You'll never understand how tough. And I'm not certain how long I can last. But the one thing I do know for certain, the only thing I'm absolutely sure of, is that I'll never have the strength to quit again."

CHAPTER FORTY-FIVE

After the orchestra's rehearsal, the musicians packed up their instruments, said their good-byes, and left the auditorium. Then Kevin handed his written notations to Julia and Irene and the three sat on the edge of the stage, feet dangling into the pit.

"Sorry it's such a scribble of notes. It's more of an outline with sections noted for improvisation. Hope you can read it."

Kevin let a few moments pass before adding, "I started this around the music of *Aida*. The tunes kept running around in my head. For some reason, I couldn't shake it, so I started composing around it, and broke the libretto down to its simplest form of three characters: a slave, a princess, and a warrior, a piece for a trio of instruments. And why not for us?"

Irene looked over the score with an eye to the parts calling for the piano solo, her head bobbing up and down as she read the allegro section.

Julie licked and pursed her lips. "Lyrical phrases for the flute."

"Yes, that's it."

Irene lifted the paper toward Kevin and pointed. "I think I understand where it calls for the gradual increase of tempo. Do you want it played with the clear themes? Here," she tapped her fingers on the page, "with the undertone of forbidden love?"

"It's yours to interpret."

Julia also brought the paper closer to Kevin. "Definite phrases of tenderness. Is that right?"

"Well, yes, definite phrases of tenderness. Perhaps a longing. And with the guitar, I hope to bring out a struggle. There should be a haunting, yet have a commanding sound culminating in power."

Irene moved to the piano while studying the notes.

Julia stood fingering her flute. "This should be fun."

Opening the clasp on the case, Kevin removed his guitar. "Shall we try it, see how it sounds?"

Irene ran her fingers up and down the keyboard, remembering how she and Kevin had first met on the plaza at Lincoln Center. Her first impression of him as a deadbeat or homeless man had been quickly corrected. Kevin was standing on the stage in front, a straightforward and seemingly accomplished man.

"Kevin, why are you so attached to *Aida*?"

"I've loved it from the first time I saw it. I was nine. I didn't want to go because my friends were all going to a birthday party at the bowling alley. But my mother forced me to accompany her, and I resented it."

He grinned and raised his chin. "I think I gave her a really hard time. I remember our seats were on the first tier, and I had to lean over to see the stage. Then the warriors and an actual a horse-drawn carriage arrived, and I was enthralled."

"That was your first opera?"

"I was hooked from that moment on. Every time I hear the music I'm back being forced to enjoy the spectacular." He laughed and nodded his head as though in agreement with himself. "For me, that opera is timeless."

Irene lifted her hands above the keyboard in readiness. "So is *Romeo and Juliet*. Neither has a happy ending."

Julia puckered her lips. Kevin nodded. The trio began.

At first it sounded like chaos, but after a few moments, the three began to sense one another, as though they'd somehow figured out a pattern, when to blend and when to shine. The piano created an undertone of intensity until the solo improvisation, when Irene let loose with split-second choices of chord upon chord. Julia's flute carried a trill, high and airy, and Kevin's rhythms continued to create tension, with his fingers flying over the melody, changing harmonies.

And when they were done, Julia threw her arms around Kevin, almost knocking him to the ground, while Irene stood looking on, clapping her hands like a child full of mischief.

"Terrific! The theme, anyone could recognize it, but it was so playful and full of rich currents, and the tension was like a speeding heartbeat. It was storytelling at its best."

Kevin held his guitar by the neck. "Much better than I ever expected. One more go-round before we leave, okay? And this time, give it your all. Julia, don't be afraid to run your trills longer, and Irene, the unexpected chords, try for more. Don't edit yourself. I'll keep the base."

Julia wiped the sweat caught in the folds of her neck and moistened the lip plate. Irene went back to the piano bench and stretched the spread of her fingers. Kevin tightened the strings on the guitar, nodded, and began again.

When they were finished, Kevin placed his guitar in the open case, then wrapped his arms around each of the girls, and ushered them out of the building onto the sidewalk, a glow of accomplishment radiating around the tight group.

They agreed to have a night cap at a café down by Lincoln Center, and the three nestled together in back seat of a cab. Kevin's aftershave lotion, a clean masculine smell, had a hint of musk, which Irene inhaled deeply. With Kevin's thigh pressed against hers, she closed her eyes to a disturbing sense of longing, a desire which seemed foreign to her recent years. Again, she felt a glimmer of possibilities.

Seated around the small table, they ordered a bottle of champagne to toast themselves and their success, and as the bubbles rose in the thin crystal glasses, tickling Irene's nose, so did her acute awareness of Kevin. She'd not been so conscious of him before tonight. Heat flooded her chest as she imagined them pressed together, her body undulating under his long fingers. Breath caught in her mouth. She wanted his arms around her. She swallowed, and thought perhaps it was simply his talent that brought on her desire.

Desirous of his touch, she placed her right elbow on the table and raised her forearm, fingers spread to their widest, and smiled an invitation. She and Kevin compared hands, palm to palm, fingers to fingers. Her hands were soft and strong and capable of octaves, and she felt his calloused fingers brush across her palm. Fingers entwined for just that one moment too long, and then the width of his palm engulfed hers, sending a shiver of pleasure. The rush of longing climbed from her chest, up her long neck, and to her cheeks, the heat causing her breath to quicken.

Embarrassed by what she knew to be bright red splotches on her face, she signaled Julia. "It's time for us to go,"

"Come on, Irene, we don't have to get up early tomorrow." Having drained the last drop from her glass, Julia licked her lips. "This can't be good for me. Alcohol is not on my diet. Anything tasting this good is a definite taboo. But what the hell, I'll have another sip, please."

Irene pushed her empty glass aside. "Tomorrow is apartment shopping, and I need an early start."

"Maybe I can help." Kevin's yes held Irene's. "It's still early. Don't go yet." Kevin refilled the three glasses with the last of the bottle. "I haven't had this much fun since…" he laughed, "can't remember when. It's been terrific to actually hear what's been playing in my head. We make beautiful music together."

There was a subtext implied by his last comment. Was she imagining it? She lifted her glass, thinking he was an easy man to like, affable and charming, the opposite of Ashford's friends, who carried chips on their shoulders as if the world owed them something. A bitter taste oozed in her mouth.

Again, she looked across the table, and saw the corners of Kevin's lips lift. He had the broad shoulders of a tennis player, and the elegance of his hand—his fingers running up and down the side of the crystal wine glass —caught her imagination. With the very thought of being held in his arms, she felt a butterfly sweep deep inside, the wings fluttering.

The flush on her face deepened. She bit her lower lip, certain he had read her private thoughts.

Kevin tipped his head ever so slightly, his eyes riveted on her. "Happy endings are always possible."

CHAPTER FORTY-SIX

Gloria dropped an olive into her martini and returned to the living room with a glass of club soda for Nick. Slinking onto the arm chair, she licked the edge of the glass, and raised it to Nick as though in a pledge. "I'll stay here until you're back on your feet. No pun intended."

"Very funny." Nick shifted on the couch, placing his bandaged foot on the cushion.

"Whether Kevin likes it or not, I'm here to take care you." Her eyelids drooped. This, her third drink of the afternoon, was taking its toll. She leaned forward to set the martini glass on the coffee table, but missed the edge, spilling the gin on the silk Persian rug.

"Oops. I remember Kevin telling me this was expensive. I never liked it to begin with." She took a tissue, got down on the floor, and dabbed at the liquid seeping into the carpet. "Kevin insisted everything remain the same. Would never hear of changing a thing. Hand me downs are not my style."

It was at that moment that Kevin came out of the elevator, moved through the entry, and placed his attaché case on the marble floor. Hearing Gloria's voice, he came into the living room and saw her on hands and knees, her blonde hair falling forward over her face. "What the hell?"

Gloria looked up at him. "Jes a little mishap."

He bent and picked up the olive and the glass, gave Gloria a hand to help her up off the floor, and then moved over next to Nick, towering over his son. "How're you feeling? Any better?"

"I'm okay."

"Are you having any pain?"

"A little, but not much."

"Headache?"

"It's gone."

Kevin looked down at the top of his son's head, his thoughts whirling with what-ifs and all the wasted years they'd been at odds with one another. The country was wide and unforgiving between the two coasts.

The time difference shouldn't have stopped him. Flights were non-stop, easy to arrange. He had barely extended the effort to visit, using Gloria and her bevy of boyfriends as his excuse. Without a role model to guide the youngster, it was no wonder he'd fallen into bad company. With a shudder, he looked over at Gloria, whose head was lolling as though there was a tune she was following.

Kevin swallowed the guilt that rose in his throat. He should have grabbed Nick by the neck and stayed on top of him until he wrung the poison from the young body. Maybe he could have straightened out the path of Nick's life, put him on a better course.

Certainly, all those years he had loved Nick, but from afar. He placed a hand gently on Nick's shoulder, and shook his head, wondering if it was too late for a father-son relationship.

"Any word from Riley?"

"Nope. Not yet."

"And her cell? Did you get any answer?"

"Nope."

"Do you think she'll come here?"

"Don't think so."

"Look, son, if she does show up, I think it would be best for everyone if she went back to California. What I mean is, I think it's best for you if she's not around," quickly adding, "it's not that I didn't like her. I did."

He turned and looked at Gloria. "I know it's hard, but everything you want is not necessarily good for you. There are choices you have to make, and they're not always easy ones."

Clasping his hands to his chest, Nick said, "I want her with me. I love her."

"Love doesn't always win."

Gloria growled. "She's finished as far as I'm concerned. A good career flushed down the toilet. If you want my two cents, it's good riddance to her. A piece of trash."

"Don't talk about her like that. She's a good person. We should be together. She just had a rough patch. She'll be okay. I know what to do. I can help her."

"I understand." Kevin bent down eye to eye with Nick. "This is really hard for you to accept, but I do truly understand. Deep down, I'll always love your mother, even through all the madness. But, you know how we are together. We bring out the worst in each other. We would destroy each other."

He rubbed his hand across his mouth, and sank down on the couch next to Nick. "Your mother is like my drug. I have to stay away from her. We can't live together."

He stood up, placed his hand on Nick's shoulder, and took a deep breath. "If you truly love Riley, if she comes here, and if you're smart and caring, you'll send her back to rehab."

CHAPTER FORTY-SEVEN

The very next morning, Irene scoured the classified listings in the newspaper, circled those rentals of interest with a red pen, and set off to find an immediate rental. As soon as she walked into the possible apartments, she was on her way out. The next day and the next week followed one after another with a futile repeat of the unfortunate hunt. She raised her price point and lowered her expectations but to no avail. Windows and sunlight and elbow room were what she looked for, but what she found on these days of her hunt were only dreary, claustrophobic apartments.

With Thanksgiving quickly approaching, pumpkins and goblins appeared in the stores with Christmas music piped in overlaying it all. Tossing away her fruitless apartment search, Irene sought a hotel room, and surprisingly found the right circumstance in a hip hotel just off Fifth Avenue.

The hotel featured a bistro off the lobby, as well as a plush cocktail lounge. In the lobby, leather club chairs were situated around low tables, creating conversation areas. Noting the clientele, Irene was reassured to see one woman reading a paperback book, a man folding back pages of the *Wall Street Journal*, a teen sitting with ear buds plugged in.

Shown to a room, Irene nodded approval even though the window of the modest bed room faced another brick building. The space was simple and clean, the bed seemed comfortable, and the bathroom properly outfitted with ample towels. Though not the luxurious surroundings Irene was familiar with, it solved her immediate problem.

Without a second thought, she arranged to stay the entire month at the hotel. After a quick trip to her bank, Irene returned, sought out the manager—a middle-aged man with ginger-bright-red hair—and paid for the full month with a cashier's check. The manager methodically ran his fingertips over the check with the greed of a fire's flame, then welcomed Irene to the hotel, giving her a key to the gym.

"If there is anything else I can do for you while you're a guest in this hotel, please ask either me or the desk clerk."

Dropping the key into her tote, she nodded. "I'll probably never use it," then turned, indicated the double doors leading to the cocktail lounge, and asked, "What time does it open?"

"Four. There's no set closing time. Midnight is usual. It appeals to a middle-aged crowd. They'd easily fall asleep at the table. You'd think this place was restricted to only those fifty and over." He laughed and with a glance at Irene, his jovial look changed on a beat.

She walked away, strode across the lobby and into the open-mouth of the elevator. The image reflected on the smoky mirror was of a worn-out woman. She could hardly believe the deep circles under her eyes, down turned mouth, hair in disarray, and the flesh on her face was puffy and pale like a mound of dough before the oven. Her cheeks twitched from the tension held in her jaw. The image reminded her of her mother.

Hands clutched to her chest, Irene said aloud, "That woman is not me."

Her focus shifted to the ceiling as the elevator began its ascent to the eleventh floor. Irene felt stunted in the small cubicle, as though she had shrunk. She no longer felt like the five feet four-inch young woman zipping around as though she owned the city. She had been shrinking, not standing straight and secure. It was no wonder the manager thought she was much older than her thirty-four years. Ashford had crushed her independence, her soul dwindling with each passing day, squeezed until the last drop fell to her husband's taunts.

She felt the motion of the elevator rising, and with a shudder it stopped on her floor. She opened her eyes wide and stared at her image, determined to never again allow her will to be squished like an ant under Ashford's cordovans, the shoes he insisted she polish each night.

The elevator door slid open, but Irene stood still, and watched until the doors closed. She pressed the lobby button, and down she went. Her reflection revealed a firm jaw and resolve sparking in the eyes. She strode back across the floor to the manager and pointed to the cocktail lounge.

"Do you have a piano in there?"

As he nodded, a lock of red hair fell forward, and he swiped it back along with a flip of his head. "Sometimes a customer gets up to play a bit. Livens up the place."

Irene stood with her feet planted firmly on the floor, wondering why she hadn't thought of this before. She'd played in her uncle's bar from the time she was a youngster. Of course, back then when she first started, the men were respectful of her youth, and each year as she grew and developed a woman's body of curves, her uncle paid a special eye to anyone who stepped out of line. Once a man put his arms around her while she was playing, his torso pressed to her spine, his hands cupping the buds of her small breasts, and wham, her uncle had him flat on the floor in no time. She'd been terrified and flattered all at the same time. That was the day she became aware of her feminine allure, and was no longer an innocent child.

Eyes sparkling, lashes wet with invention, she leaned across the reception desk "Want to hire me as a pianist for a few hours a night?"

"You?"

"Sure. Me."

"You play?"

"Try me tonight."

"There's nothing in the budget."

"Whatever business you have now will certainly increase with live music."

As the manager rolled his fingers on the desk, Irene noted the bitten nails.

"Maybe we can swap. I'll increase your business, and you let me use of the piano when the lounge is not open."

"Don't think so."

"That piano is just sitting dormant all day long."

"To do what?"

"Practice and teach. With me playing popular songs when the lounge is open, your business will flourish. It's a win-win."

Irene could almost see the wheels of his brain stirring, the stem of a watch turning, the inside of his mouth filling with saliva. The freckles on his nose darkened when he placed his forearms on the desk and leaned forward. "Maybe you should pay."

Irene took a step back, a smile crinkling at the corner of her eyes. "Think of tonight as an audition, and if it all works out, it'll be good for both of us."

"What's in it for me?"

"Ten percent of my tips."

"Twenty."

"Twenty it is." Irene nodded in agreement, and marched with purpose across the lobby. Pushing open the double glass doors to the lounge, she whispered, "New beginnings."

CHAPTER FORTY-EIGHT

Nick adjusted his pillow, rolled onto his side, and lay watching the illuminated minutes pass on the face of his watch. He counted the minutes, the hours and days creeping by ever since the night he'd left Riley retching in the cheap hotel bathroom. Though his foot had healed and the last of the bandages removed, the ache he endured remained not in the bones or tendons but in his chest. With each breath he took, the guilt he carried was fresh.

Retracing the steps they'd taken that night, Nick squeezed his eyes closed to revisit the scene. It began at the drug store and the stolen meds, went on to Rays Pizza, and the two of them holding hands and strolling the dark night until she opened her hand with the pills. Denying his own temptation, he had pleaded with her to throw away the drugs, but she'd downed the handful almost out of spite, or maybe even a dare. They'd gone on to the club, had drinks and danced, alone and together, her hips gyrating, her hands running up and down his body, and then flying apart. The dimly light dance floor was crowded and noisy, impossible to hear one another over the music from the DJ's pounding bass.

He'd lost sight of Riley until he spotted her leaning against a man, her hips pressed against his, writhing in a sexual joining. He dragged Riley away, her eyes wild, hitting him and yelling, staggering up the stairs in the cheap hotel, vomiting obscenities, then passing out on a bare mattress. He could barely remember loving her. Where had the vows and trust gone? At rehab, they'd leaned on each other. She'd been the steady tower holding him upright, been the stabilizing influence. He thought of her as a pillar in rehab, now crumbled and fallen. He wanted her clean. Never should he have left her. He punched his pillow again and again.

The irresistible smell of bacon roused Nick from bed, a cocoon from which he hadn't risen all week. Stumbling into the kitchen, he was surprised to see Kevin with his hand deep in the cavity of a huge turkey. Large mixing bowls were spread on the counter top, stalks of celery and mounds of onions lay topsy-turvy. Two cookbooks were open to dog-eared pages, while the laptop showed another recipe.

"Grab a fork and turn the bacon."

"I like bacon straight." Nick took thongs from the drawer and turned over each piece, the fat sputtering. "That bird looks big enough to feed an army."

"Gloria ordered a twenty-eight-pound fresh turkey for Thanksgiving dinner. She should be here doing this. As usual, she's late. Nick, look at this book and then the web." He indicated with a nod while his hands probed for the giblets. "One recipe says dressing and one gives directions for stuffing."

"Which one asks for bacon?"

"This one," He pointed with his chin to the laptop. "And oysters. Gloria's supposed to bring them. And what's the difference between minced and diced onions?" Confusion clustered around his eyes, the tiny scar turned crimson as he opened the bag of turkey giblets, the neck curling around his hand. "What are we supposed to do with this?"

"Dad, you're out of your element. Let me take over."

"Happily."

Kevin, nudged out of the way, smiled and patted the turkey's breast. Hands held up as a surgeon, he turned toward the sink and scrubbed just as the intercom rang announcing Gloria's arrival.

With a burst of perfume and packages, Gloria, charging ahead on her spike heels, crossed the marble floor and into the kitchen, where she dumped the bags on the floor. She handed a garment bag to Nick. "Hang this in the closet. I don't want it wrinkled. And you need a shower."

"And good morning to you." He grabbed the cleaner's plastic bag and limped from the kitchen.

"He smells like he just got up."

"He did. A couple of minutes ago."

Gloria turned to Kevin. "I don't know why you allow him to stay in bed for days on end, not get up and out to find a job."

"Go easy, Gloria. He's just now back on his feet. Recuperation took time."

She wagged her forefinger in front of his face. "Trying to be the good father after all this time?" She sidled up to Kevin, grabbed him around the waist, pulled him to her, and pressed her lips on his neck, then nibbled the warm flesh. Running her palm down the front of his trousers, her gravelly voice whispered, "Time to get the bird in the hot oven."

"Is sex always on your mind?"

She leaned back and looked him full in the face while she smoothed her palms across his chest. "Is that so bad? You seemed to like it."

"Gloria," he gripped her wrists, pressed them to his mouth, and kissed the inside tender spots. "That was a long long time ago."

"You can't fool me. I know you too well. You still want me. Your body answers to mine. I can feel it rising." She backed away, put on a white chef's apron, and leaned against the counter, shaking her forefinger with a broad smile crinkling her dancing eyes. "Once this turkey gets in the oven, we will have hours together to discuss our future. But for now, grab the chef's knife and cut up the vegetables."

Acknowledging that Gloria still held strings to his life, Kevin glanced out of the window, thinking the parade should have a Pinocchio balloon with his face painted on it. Gloria had a tenacious pull he could not shake, no matter what he had done over the years to amputate his love of her. As he stood gazing from his apartment window, he thought it odd that though Gloria had been with numerous men, he never felt a single shred of jealousy. He wondered if what he had felt was love and now simply a kind of loss.

He rested his forehead on the window pane, remembering the pain he felt at her leaving him twenty years ago with the baby snuggled in her arms. At random times, he could hear her husky voice, whether during the day or at night when he turned off the light. Sometimes he could hear her exact words. "I will remember you, but you will never forget me." It was an odd thing for her to have said, but it had the ring of truth.

Gloria snapped the laptop closed, pushed the recipe book out of the way, and tore open the packages she'd left on the floor. With a sigh, pushing back from the window, Kevin watched her slip off her bright red stilettos and toss them toward the dining room. He moved back from the window with a shrug, wiped his hands on a paper towel, threw it in the garbage pail, and grabbed a knife, onions, and celery.

Later, while the turkey roasted in the oven and the smell of a Thanksgiving feast wafted throughout the apartment, Gloria went into the master bedroom, calling back to Kevin, "I'll be in the shower waiting for you."

Avoiding a possible scene, Kevin went into his library, and with a firm hand, closed the door. Sitting at his desk, the computer monitor sprang to life with a nudge of the mouse. He opened a spreadsheet, and casually perused the up-to-date accounting of his many buildings and holdings. His eyes ran down the figures of the database, stopped, and rolled back to one of his apartment buildings. He leaned in closer to the screen and clicked to a new screen. Opening before him was the year-end statement for his favorite building, where he himself owned several apartments. His attention focused on a shortness of funds in the reserve. The figures made no sense to Kevin. None of his holdings had ever run a deficit.

He tapped the little scar on his forehead, his mind settling on only one good reason for this shortage: the board of directors was not fulfilling their fiduciary responsibilities. Kevin scrolled down further knowing that the president of that condo board was none other than Ashford Aubrey.

CHAPTER FORTY-NINE

Not wanting to intrude on Julia's time with her sister, Irene had turned down the invitation to join them in celebration of Thanksgiving, and had gone by herself to a diner for turkey dinner. The streets were crowded with families who had watched the parade, children carrying balloons, jackets flying open as they skipped down the sidewalk, their parents close behind. Irene stood and watched one child, snot running from her red nose, being shaken by an adult.

She remembered her father grabbing her shoulders when she spilled her milk on the linoleum kitchen floor and shaking the living daylights out of her frail six-year-old body. She was so rattled she'd bit her tongue. Ice held in her mouth had not stopped the bleeding, and her new white sneakers never again looked clean, the dark smudge stayed until they were outgrown. Irene wanted to pull the woman aside, tell her to talk to the child, not scare the youngster with physical abuse, but resisted the temptation.

Though alone, Irene felt completely at peace with herself. She'd made great progress in finding a place to rest her head, no matter that it was only a small hotel room, and a possible income playing piano. All she had to do now was advertise, spread the word, and publicize the lounge as the place to enjoy an evening with friends and loved ones.

Surprisingly, the diner was not empty, but swarming with lost souls, the atmosphere buzzing with commonality. On a seat at the counter, she sat between a roly-poly double for Santa Claus and a very tall man clad in black who could have starred in film as an undertaker. Someone put coins in the old jukebox. It didn't take long before the single voice of Bing Crosby was joined by others singing "Count Your Blessings." The diners, from old to young, ancient to babies, all seemed to feel the camaraderie of joining in thanks. It didn't matter that the turkey was not hot and the gravy was thin, the marshmallows hadn't melted on the sweet potatoes, and the peas were straight from a can.

Irene sang along with the crowd, laughing with such a gleeful group, and scraped her fork at the bottom of her desert dish having devoured a surprisingly delicious, cinnamon filled apple pie a la mode. She wiped her chin. A baby girl, bundled in pink, was held high by the proud father, the tenor voice of a short older man with pudgy cheeks rang true to pitch, and Irene joined in the merriment with the clear voice of a soprano.

Good cheer, bursting from the windows and doors, was hard to hold inside the diner, and a group of mismatched celebrants, arm in arm, made their way out of the restaurant and down the street, heading directly toward the hotel. Irene in the lead guided them through the front entrance and into the lounge, where she quickly went to the piano and picked up the tune of "It's a Wonderful World." Soon the song became an ode to Thanksgiving, and her new friends rose to their feet and clustered around the piano. Waiters and bartenders, towels slung over their arms, jumped into action.

Voices following the piano's guidance streamed into one song after another, flooding the hotel lobby with gaiety and tunes that soared into the street beckoning others to join. The lounge overflowed with customers, and soon empty glasses were refilled with drinks, and tips poured into the gratuity basket. Feeling as though she had awakened from a deep sleep, Irene's blood raced to her fingertips. Her heart beat a steady rhythm and when she took a break to catch her breath and have a glass of wine, she called Julia to share her good news, saying "all's well with the world."

CHAPTER FIFTY

Gloria dimmed the overhead lights while Kevin struck a match to the long-tapered candles set in ornate silver candle sticks on the table. They flickered for a moment until steady flames illuminated the dining room. A slight limp remained in Nick's gait when he came in, pulled out his chair, and flopped onto it.

Gloria smoothed her palms down the sides of her slinky silk dress. "Honestly, Nick, this is Thanksgiving dinner. The least you could do was dress properly."

"You can hardly see what I'm wearing, it's so dark in here. What difference does it—"

"Respect for me and your father. That's what."

"What the hell. Suddenly we're so proper?"

Gloria's emerald eyes caught a sparkle of candle light. "It's never too late to start again. Right, Kevin? This is a new beginning for the three of us. We're all together to—"

The sound of the buzzer interrupted Gloria's rehearsed speech. "Who the hell is that?"

Kevin went into the front hall and picked up the intercom. When the concierge announced Riley, Kevin stiffened, and without any hesitation told the concierge not to allow her entry. As though there was nothing out of the ordinary, he went back into the dining room and sat down. "Sorry for the interruption."

"What was that all about?"

"Just business."

"On a holiday?"

"Forget it. Just a package, and I told the doorman not to deliver it."

"On a holiday! You should tell your office to leave you alone on a holiday. I want you all to myself... and Nick, of course." She reached toward Kevin and tugged his forearm.

Kevin pulled his arm back and sat stiffly on his chair at the head of the table.

Nick drummed his fingers on the Irish linen tablecloth.

Gloria leaned forward, picked up the decanter, and poured chilled Chateau Lanessan into the crystal wine glasses.

Nick pushed his glass aside. "Not for me."

"Sweetheart. A tiny sip won't do you any harm."

"Leave him alone."

"What do you mean by that?"

"You hover over Nick. Let him breathe!"

"What's gotten into you?" She served the endive salad topped with crab meat. "Nick, tell your father I don't 'hover'."

Kevin, full of his own thoughts, twirled the wine around in the goblet, then sipped without tasting. Had he overstepped his rights as a father to protect his son? Perhaps, he thought, he should have gone down to the lobby and sent Riley directly to a rehab center where she belonged. He imagined Nick being drawn back to her, remembered how they sat so close to one another, their foreheads touching. Drugs were not on his radar right now. Who knew what her influence would be if she were to come back into his life. He might be pulled down with her, down, down into that deep well of drugs.

With an abrupt motion, Kevin pushed himself back from the table. "Excuse me. There's something I have to do." He strode out of the room, down the hall to the elevator. Barely waiting for the doors to slide open at the lobby, he saw the doorman posted near the wide glass doors, and the concierge standing behind the tall entry desk. Then he spotted Riley sitting demurely on a couch in the alcove, a shawl wrapped around her shoulders. As he came closer he saw her face was pale with sunken cheeks, and her spiky hair, now dyed blue, was cut close to her head.

Her lips were pinched as she nodded. "I wondered if you'd come. Did you tell Nick I was here?"

"No."

"I didn't think you would." She rubbed her palms on her thighs. "If I was in your shoes, I wouldn't have."

Looking up to the ornate ceiling, Kevin said, "Nick is not strong enough to be in a relationship with you." He shook his head and looked directly at her sunken eyes, remembering when he first saw her, the nude silhouette standing in front of the window, the moon light casting a milky outline of her sensuous young body.

He cleared his throat, thrusting aside the memory. "I can't let you bring him down again. He's tried too many times to be rid of the habit and failed, but this time, I thought this time was different. He had you as a steady sober influence. You know that's no longer the case!"

"You're right."

He reached into his pocket for his wallet. "Do you have a place to go? Do you need—"

The corners of her lips tilted upward, and she put her hand on his arm. "A girl like me always has a place to go." She stood. "I only came for my clothes."

They stood facing one another, his tall athletic frame, strong and firm; her supple body swaying slightly. "I really did like him, you know."

"I'll have your things packed up. Where should they be sent?"

"I'll let you know." She walked away with an elegance reminiscent of young Gloria, hips swaying as though to a tune in her head. He watched her turn, wave a good-bye as the doorman opened the heavy glass doors letting in a gust of cold air, and disappear into the night.

Inside the elevator, Kevin leaned against the back wall, thinking of the similarities between Gloria and Riley: both self-absorbed, sensual women, using sex as a commodity. Kevin waited a moment after the doors opened onto his apartment, then strode through the entry, down the hall, into the kitchen.

"Where did you go in the middle of Thanksgiving dinner? I worked really hard to prepare for this just for your benefit." Gloria stood wielding a long knife and fork over the roast turkey

"I had to take care of something."

"What was so important you had to leave us?"

"Nothing of your concern."

"On a holiday like this, only family counts. Nothing else." She wagged the knife at Kevin, then put it on the counter. She smiled and arched her back, her breasts pressed forward, straining in the taut burnt-orange dress. She raised an eyebrow, took a step closer, and placed her palms on his hot cheeks.

"Stop it."

Her hands were clutching him, her fingers leaches digging into his flesh, draining him dry. He pulled her hands from him.

"Was it a woman?"

"Don't do this, Gloria. It's not a concern of yours."

"Darling, everything you do is a concern of mine."

Kevin, for the first time in their entire relationship, looked at the woman standing in his kitchen and felt nothing. Not a twinge of desire or longing. He felt absolutely nothing. At long last, he was free of Gloria.

CHAPTER FIFTY-ONE

The secretary ushered Irene into the conference room. Her attorney, Peter Sheehy, sat at the head of a vast walnut table circled by a dozen matching chairs. Irene scanned the sunlit room outfitted with accessories of black leather and shiny ebony. There were legal size pads alongside silver pens on the table, and one wall consisted of legal reference books neatly aligned from floor to ceiling, enough pomp to instill awe, her nerves sending sparks of alarm.

The attorney indicated a swivel chair next to him, then folded his hands on top of a thick file. His bowtie was partly covered by fleshy jowls, and his snow-white hair curled up at his collar. He cast an eye at his watch. "There's nothing to be nervous about. This is a preliminary step to see where we stand with the divorce. I trust this meeting can be held without any emotional outburst. It's simply a place to start. Simple."

"Simple? Nothing involving Ashford is ever simple."

"I'm pleased they acknowledged the need for this meeting. Until now, Mr. Aubrey has been very evasive. They should be along any moment now."

Irene sat with her back straight and strong, her shoulders set in granite, and her mouth was dry as a barren creek. Barely able to lick her lips, she was grateful for the silver pitcher of water placed on the table. She reached for a glass, but her hands shook so badly that the attorney reached out and poured the water into a tumbler.

The cold water was such a relief, that Irene gulped several mouthfuls. But seeing Ashford following the secretary into the room, she choked on the water, spewing a stream onto the conference table. Coughing and struggling to regain her decorum, Irene reached for the tissue box to mop the conference table. A red flush heated her chest and neck, setting her cheeks on fire as though she had been strangled.

"That's my wife for you, always creating a scene." His mocking voice accompanied a sneer as he took a seat directly across from Irene. Without any hesitation he introduced himself to the attorney, saying, "I'll be representing myself. Shall we get started?"

The attorney took a moment before he replied. "That's not advisable. Shall we adjourn until you decide on—"

"No need to postpone this meeting. I am well equipped with a heartfelt offer to carry on as Irene's husband and welcome her back without any recriminations." He tilted his head and blinked in the manner of a comedian with raised eyebrows and eyes wide open, the pupils black as a coal mine. "Take my word, there will be no accusations or reproach if my offer today is taken. Otherwise, and Irene knows this only too well, I'll eat her alive."

"This is highly irregular."

Irene took a long breath through flaring nostrils, and leaned across the table. "You actually expect me to stay married to you?"

"Of course."

"Not for one more moment will I live with you."

"And you expected me to allow a divorce, declare our marriage over? Just what did you expect, Irene?"

"Mr. Aubrey, that's what we are here to discuss: an equitable compromise for both parties. Otherwise, we will all end up in a court battle that will take money and time. Mr. Aubrey, I'm certain, as an attorney, you are aware of the legalities involved in a marital dispute ending in court."

"As my own attorney, I welcome the battle. I'm certain from the papers Irene had copied, and of which you are now in possession," he indicated the file resting on the table with the thrust of his chin, "you have taken note that there is a signed prenuptial agreement?"

Irene gripped her hands together. Her anger flared, but she held herself in check, tightening the tendons around her mouth. "You know I never signed that."

"You need psychiatric care."

The attorney pulled a sheet of paper from his file and laid it in front of Mr. Aubrey. "I have had a handwriting expert view this signature, and he has determined, this is not your wife's handwriting."

Ashford looked at the declaration, then took from his breast pocket a folded paper and laid that in front of the attorney. "And I have my expert stating unequivocally that it is." He reached into the pocket of his jacket and pulled out a small bag of pistachio nuts. "What is it we used to call it when we were kids? Oh," the sneer on his face deepened to menacing at the curl of his upper lip. "Tit for tat. Yes, that's it." One by one, Ashford sat cracking open the shells and popping the nuts into his mouth.

Mr. Sheehy pulled another group of papers from the file. "Here, this is a draft of what we deem is fair and equitable. You'll see it includes real property as well as a cash settlement, a fair share of stock, and some personal items. After all the years of marriage, this is the very least your wife deserves."

Ashford ran his forefinger down one page after another, until he took up the papers, shredded them into little pieces, and threw them into the air as confetti. "If you think for one bloody second that I will support this leftover lump of a woman, you are suffering a terrible delusion." Then he bolted out of his chair and lunged at Irene. "Get this straight, you piece of shit: I will never grant you a divorce."

So filled with anger, Irene's teeth hurt down to the root, her scalp itched, and bile rose to the back of her mouth. She smelled his rage, and grasped the edge of the table to secure herself.

"There's no need for name-calling, Mr. Aubrey" the attorney interrupted. He leaned toward Ashford as he opened another file. "Here are other issues worthy of mentioning at this time. These trusts, signed by you, appear to have been mishandled, funds misappropriated. Would I be too forward in suggesting you would not want this taken any further than my professional instincts?"

"How dare you imply—"

"Perhaps a better word choice would be embezzlement."

"That I would pocket—"

"Is it true?" Irene's forehead wrinkled, and her lips pinched. "Have you been helping yourself to funds that belong to other people, your own clients? Tell me, is that where all the money came from?"

"This is an outrage." His eyes flicked to Irene and seemed to spark with the fire of evil. "You hired this pompous, misdirected, mudslinging old man. I'll sue him for, for…"

"We'll see you in court." The attorney riffled through the many pages, while a satisfied look crept onto his face.

Ashford punched his fist on the table. "You wouldn't!"

The attorney let a few seconds lumber by. "This is not a dare, Mr. Aubrey. I'm merely pointing out my instincts for justice. The legal system will want a good accounting of your various trusts with deceased individuals. Perhaps only a reimbursement of what's been siphoned off the families will be required of you."

He sat back and placed his palms on the open files. "My advice? Hire a top-notch attorney. That is, unless, you would like to put the whole issue behind by agreeing to the divorce and settlement we are proposing." Again, Mr. Sheehy drew papers from a file, and placed the fresh documents on the solid walnut conference table. He handed Ashford one of the silver pens lying in readiness. He smiled at Irene. "Of course, my client will sign an agreement of confidentiality, and the matter will be a closed book."

The normal shroud of bullying tactics seemed to slide from Ashford's shoulders. He slumped in his chair. Irene saw by his cold eyes that it was true: he had been cheating his clients. Revealing this would be his ruination. Yet, it brought her no satisfaction. Instead, a sense of guilt enveloped Irene. She bit the inside of her cheek. Never wanting, she had enjoyed the big house, the designer clothing, theater and restaurants, all the luxuries money could buy. Unknowingly, she had gladly partaken of Ashford's fraudulent lifestyle.

She looked down at her limp hands, and then squeezed her eyes closed. She had no right to the cash she had squirreled away each week. The money in her safe deposit box belonged to others.

CHAPTER FIFTY-TWO

Kevin took a towel from his gym bag, wiped the sweat from his forehead, dabbed the grip of his tennis racket, slung the damp towel around his neck, and headed for the showers with no time for the steam room. Preoccupied with thoughts of the evening, he dressed quickly, went home to grab his guitar, and rode a cab up town just in time for rehearsal.

In the auditorium, he searched the orchestra already seated on the stage. Disappointed to see that it was not Irene at the piano, his eyes went to the wind section and saw Julia. Fiddling with the clasps on the guitar case, it fell open, and he grasped the instrument by the neck. Rubbing the fingerboard along the frets, he climbed the few steps, took his place on the stage, gave Julia a questioning look, and received a shrug in response.

The orchestra tuned up with a cacophony of sound until all settled on the oboe's note of A. A strained silence filled the stage of musicians with nervous anticipation as the conductor tapped his baton on the music stand. "While playing this unusual interpretation of Ravel's ballet, keep in mind, this is a romantic tale." Again, he tapped the stand, raised both arms to begin a shortened rendition of *Daphnis et Chloe*.

After a few rough starts, the melody came true, the tender music related to the Greek myth of young love. It sounded peaceful in its simplicity until the music rose in volume and complexity. Kevin waited for his small part, and as he turned pages of the score, his mind wandered to *Aida* and her unrequited love for a soldier she could never have. In a flash he could almost hear a flute and clarinet bring forth emotions of pity, ending in a crescendo, a finale of blaring trumpets. Aida never wanted pity.

Kevin played his small part without enthusiasm. His mind wandered, and he imagined Irene. He wondered at his disappointment in her not being at this rehearsal. He didn't know much about the woman. He wanted to know more. Certainly, she was pleasant. Good looking. A very fine pianist. She had set upon his original score with an appetite for innovation, and had played his piece with brilliance. The improvisational parts sang, and Kevin had to admit he was quite flattered at her attention.

Glancing around the orchestra, Kevin's eyes stopped at the first violinist, whose face showed utter self-absorption as he tapped the score with the tip of his bow. The man was so full of himself that he practically ignored the other musicians. Kevin looked at Julia holding her flute delicately. His thoughts circled back to Irene. She was not in the least self-aggrandizing. There was something honest in her character, quite the opposite of Gloria.

At the end of rehearsal, the conductor seemed pleased with the results. He nodded to all the participants. He shook hands with Kevin, a two-handed grip which brought to Kevin's mind a handshake, a remembrance, not forgotten, but one he had buried. It was a single moment that came with a crushing gulp of air. His mother sat close to him, squeezing his shoulder, and she was weeping in a quiet way he'd never heard before. His tiny hand was engulfed by two withered hands. All bone and blue veins popping just under the skin.

Kevin could still feel those hands. Nearby, there was an insistent, slow beeping sound. The scent of mothballs was pervasive. The old man's whiskers were rough against his young cheek. The voice wheezed and sprayed spittle. "You're the man of the house, now."

Kevin blinked to close off the memory of himself, a three-year-old, adrift with only his mother to guide him, raised with the wealth of past generations, but not a single male to nurture him. He had made his way out from under his mother's grasp, but only after she died.

On his way out of the rehearsal, he gave Julia a hug. "How come Irene's not here? I was hoping we'd play my piece again tonight."

"Oh, she couldn't make it."

"Shame. I wanted to give my piece a go again. I can't seem to shake it from my mind. I have to laugh at myself. I even named it."

"Really?"

"I call it "After Aida." Silly isn't it?"

"Not at all."

"We can play it after the next rehearsal. If she's here, that is."

"She's got a gig playing piano at a lounge."

"Every night?"

"I think so. It's attached to the hotel where she's been staying. She said the place is jumping. In just a few weeks, she's gotten a large following, thank God for that." She shook her head and said, "Entre-nous, her divorce has not been going so well."

"That's too bad."

"It's really upsetting. You know, she lived a very high lifestyle. That was on the outside. Inside, she was the definition of an abused woman."

"Didn't know that."

"And now that she's finally gathered enough courage to leave the bastard, her soon-to-be-her-ex-husband has managed to knock everything out from under her."

"She seems very put-together."

"That's on the outside…"

Walking together out of the building, Kevin stopped suddenly, putting his hand on her arm. "Why don't we go have a drink at the lounge where she's playing? You know the place?"

"You mean now?"

"Why not!"

CHAPTER FIFTY-THREE

The crowded lounge was in need of a facelift, if not a deep cleaning. Customers stood three deep at the long bar. Kevin scanned the room filled with mismatched tables, old fashioned chairs, some with torn leather seats. The wood floor showed deep grooves of wear, but the mood created by Irene at the piano was one of youthful gaiety. A group was clustered around the piano singing the Beatles song, "Yellow submarine." Raucous laughter from people at two tables pushed together, seemed like one big house fraternity party. Drinks were flowing. Waiters juggled round trays of drinks and simple bar food, the remnants remaining on small plates left here and there.

Kevin caught Irene's attention with a wave, and then helped Julia take off her jacket while she clung to her flute case. Kevin squeezed past several tables and hung the jacket on the clothes tree in the corner. With no seating available, they stayed close to the door through the next two songs: "Sweet Caroline," was followed by a loud version of "I love Rock and Roll" with stomping and earsplitting voices sung out from all directions. After that, Irene played a running series of chords, and the crowded room quieted.

"She's got the crowd eating out of her hand."

"Hi to you all tonight. A hearty welcome." Irene's eyes sparkled with a brilliance matched by the sequins on the plum-colored sweater she wore. She stood with one hand daintily stroking the piano's ivories, the other hand waving Kevin and Julia forward.

Julia whispered to Kevin, "What's she up to?"

"Beats me." Hearing himself say those words, he drew back, thinking he sounded just like his son, but his concentration flew back to Irene.

"Some of you here tonight have already become regulars—"

There was a smattering of applause. Julia nudged Kevin to clap.

An older man with grey dread-locks slammed his glass down on the bar. "Another!"

The rumbling of an argument arose from two young couples at a table near the corner. "Shut it!" He pointed and stuck his finger inches from the other guy's face.

"Up yours."

"Forget it, man." The other shrugged.

"And fuck you, too."

"Get on with it," a man shouted from near the door.

Irene raised both palms in an effort to quiet the fracas, which had all the earmarks of a squall. Her face held an appreciative smile, and with a little bob of her head, she continued. "With Christmas fast approaching, here's a gift packaged by my close friends, the musicians Julia and Kevin. I'm sure with a bit of encouragement, they will join me with a bit of jazz for your enjoyment."

"I Wanna Hold Your Hand," a shout from the same table.

"Keep it down," a heavy woman hissed at them.

"Mind your own business, fat face."

The woman's husband half-rose, his shiny bald head turned toward the young man. "What did you just say to my wife?"

"Nothing, Asshole."

"Apologize to my wife."

The young man curled his upper lip and slowly rose from his chair, bowed, and in a mocking voice, said. "Is there any way I can graciously say I'm sorry?" He bent, and thrust his face forward, as though studying the woman's visage. Then he flung his arms into the air, laughed, and said, "No, she does have a fat face." Those at his boisterous table joined the laughter.

The husband bolted upright, his chair falling back onto the next table. He grabbed the young man's shoulder with a firm grip. "Listen to me, you arrogant, self-indulgent child."

Shaking off the grasp, the young man whirled around with his right arm raised in a boxer's stance, and shouted. "Take your fucking hand off of me!"

Kevin moved as a panther, quick on his feet and silent in his approach. He shoved both men apart, keeping them at arm's distance.

"There's no need for this. Both of you take it easy. Sit down and enjoy the rest of the evening."

"Bastard," muttered the bald man, jutting up his chin. His hands flexed, and he glared at the young man.

"That's enough, you two. Settle down."

The young man laughed, and gave the bald man the finger.

The bald man shrugged at his jacket, trying to get it off. His chest pushed against Kevin's restraint. He shouted, "Lick my balls!"

The young man swung his fist, but missed his target, smashing Kevin's nose. Kevin staggered backward. Customers bolted aside. People yelled. The bald man bent and rammed the young man in the stomach. People shouted. Chairs scraped. Tables overturned. Plates and glasses crashed. Blood streamed down Kevin's face. He fell onto a chair, grabbed a napkin, and held it to his nose.

Seized by two waiters, the young man was dragged outside and dumped on the sidewalk. The bald man and his heavy wife left of their own accord. A few patrons sat back as though undisturbed by the commotion. Those at the bar turned back around to their drinks, while a middle-aged couple grabbed their coats and left without paying the tab.

Julia was frozen in place, while Irene rushed to Kevin's side with a towel and ice. She held the cold pack against his nose. Her face had lost its color, though the sparkle in her eyes had not faded.

"Whatever possessed you to do that?"

"I didn't want you to lose your job—"

"I wouldn't have."

"—or expose you to a barroom brawl."

"I've seen a few." She tilted his head back and adjusted the icepack. When Kevin placed his hand over hers, she inhaled his masculine scent of musk.

"Thanks for the ice."

"My uncle would have used a beefsteak."

He removed the towel from his face, squinted his eyes, and squeezed his thumb and forefinger on the bridge of his nose. "I don't think it's broken."

"It's almost stopped bleeding." Her body was leaning toward him, her eyes absorbing the eyebrows, the shadow below his hair line, and the partly open lips. She could hear his breath going in and out, and she felt herself breathing in unison.

A smile caused the tiny creases at the corners of his eyes to deepen, his mouth turning up in an endearing grin. "I can't believe I did that."

"Neither can I." A nervous laugh she tried to suppress made its way out of Irene's throat. She put her palm over her mouth. "Sorry. But that belonged in a movie somewhere with Sylvester Stallone."

"Yeah. Big time hero gets his due." He clasped her hand again, and brought the ice pack to his face. He kept hold of her hand, pressing it on his cheek. He focused on Irene's eyes and the warmth that surrounded her. "If it didn't hurt, I'd laugh with you. Ridiculous of me, a man twice their age."

"Surprised yourself!"

Their eyes had locked on each other as Kevin stroked her hand. Though his fingers were calloused from the guitar strings, Irene felt their desire. There was a sustained moment of longing that fluttered like the wings of a butterfly inside Irene. She'd thought only teenagers felt that way.

CHAPTER FIFTY-FOUR

Once turkey leftovers were placed between slices of bread, the carcass either thrown in the garbage or into a pot of simmering water, all prayers for Thanksgiving were drowned in a wave of Christmas spirit. Mother Nature was tuned to the calendar with an instant drop of thirty degrees. The icy wind of a nor'easter roared around each street corner.

Kevin walked slowly past department stores windows displaying finery with tinsel and evergreen branches, silver bells and shiny ribbons. Crowds of tourists blocked the sidewalks. He watched children wide-eyed in front of the displays, clapping hands in front of fairy-book characters and a carousel of animals set free. But his favorite was the winter wonderland with snowmen dancing and a train chugging up the hill saying, "I think I can, I think I can."

The window brought to mind a package with bright red ribbons tied around shiny green paper. His Christmas gift, wrapped with care, was a special book about the little engine that could. The pages were full of colorful illustrations, and while his mother read the book to him, he pointed to words here and there, understanding the written letters at the age of two. She tousled his hair. "My little man, you're smart as a whip."

His mother wasted no time telling everyone that he was an early reader, headed for greatness. Throughout the holiday seasons she dragged him from one party to another, keeping him tied to her side. And when he was a bit older, his mother insisted he wear a scratchy overcoat. It was styled for an old man. "My king among men," he heard his mother's whisper rush in the wind at the countdown of a new year. The words on his mother's breath tunneled in the air, "you're a one in a million." He was her shining knight in a custom-made tuxedo.

His mind wandered to the little sailor suit he was not allowed to wear to church. His first woolen pants and button-down shirt separating him from his friends, who were allowed to kick around in khaki pants and sweatshirts. Set apart throughout his years of private schools, college, and his degrees, he'd been an easy mark for Gloria.

Kevin zig-zagged his way over to Madison Avenue and his office. The holiday season was meant to be joyous. For Kevin, this time of year meant a round of office parties, dinner engagements, and cocktail parties. Invitations flooded his mailbox. Both social and business requirements, Kevin forced himself to attend each and every one. He hated the false gaiety, but was obliged to attend.

Tearing open yet another invitation, late one morning he phoned Irene. "Glad I caught you."

"I'm just on my way out." She took her coat from the closet and tossed it on the hotel bed.

"I need a favor." He should have started this conversation in an entirely different manner, should have simply asked her for a date, but once started, he proceeded to beg her to join him on the merry-go-round of parties.

"I know, I sound child-like, but please, please, please come with me this Wednesday afternoon."

"Anything interesting?"

"Just know that I need you to come with me."

"What's this all about? Or do you intend to keep me in the dark?"

"You'll be my protector."

"Ha, since when do you need protection?"

"From all those she-wolves at holiday parties. I'm forever being introduced as the wealthy bachelor who remains unattached. Every year, it's the same scenario. Single women think nothing of thrusting their phone numbers into my hand, and depositing lipstick smears on both cheeks. I feel like the prize bull."

"Doesn't seem so terrible that you can't handle it alone."

"I'm left making up excuses year after year. You can't imagine what it's like."

"Sounds like you're being pursued."

"Come with me. Just for one day, and you'll see what I mean. It's overkill with sumptuous food and drink and local gossip. This entire month of December is gobbled up with mindless small talk and the issuing of gratuities. Everyone has their hand out."

"Do you have to go to all these office parties?"

"My business requires it. It's something I have to do. It's expected of me."

"There's something wrong performing like a puppet, always doing what's expected. I know that feeling, like bowing to those who are in control of your daily life." She crossed her ankles and slid low on her chair.

"I simply have to show my face."

"You don't seem to like doing this very much."

"I don't, but it's hard to break the pattern. I was raised to be social and competitive."

"Obligations can eat up the better part of a life. You know, it's never too late to change."

She squinted against the bright morning light shining through the window, and straightened in her chair with the awkward sense of having just been audacious, handing out advice that she had herself just started to effectuate.

"Except for doling out bonuses, I hate the pretense of all this Christmas partying. It's a charade."

"Then don't do it."

"Wish I could."

"Surely you can. Go on a trip. Break the pattern. Get out of town."

"Escape?"

There was silent moment before Irene chuckled to herself. "No one should ever be trapped."

CHAPTER FIFTY-FIVE

Kevin and Irene braved the fierce winds until Kevin was able to flag down a cab. Once they were squeezed into the backseat, Irene peered out of the streaked window at shoppers hefting bags, sightseers with cameras slung around their padded shoulders, office workers hurrying home pushing through the crowds, woolen scarves wrapped about their faces. Cabs lurched and sped through yellow lights, the sound of raucous horns mixing with the insistence of the Salvation Army bells.

As the cab screeched across the avenue, Irene was flung across the seat, and though she tried to keep herself upright, her shoulders and hips shifted, bumping her onto Kevin's solid frame. She laughed, as did he. Once the cab stopped, she sat upright, Kevin paid the driver, and they stepped from the cab. The doorman bowed to Kevin and opened the heavy glass door of the building. Then he stood to the side.

Kevin pulled an envelope from the chest pocket of his overcoat and handed it to the doorman. "Merry Christmas."

"Thank you, Mr. Brooks."

"A well-deserved bonus."

"Sir. I know you saved my job for me this year, and I thank you."

"As long as I manage this building, you can depend on a job here."

"I'm most grateful. Thank you, sir." The doorman nodded. "The party is being held in the reception room this year."

Irene, hands deep in her coat pockets, waited with Kevin just a moment for the elevator to arrive and hoist them upward to the penthouse. When the doors slid open, Irene stumbled from the elevator into the heavy fog of evergreen. A butler took her cashmere coat and whisked it to a rack. Irene put her hand to her chest and waited for Kevin who stood in the elevator until the doors began to close on him. She watched him take a gulp of air and step to her side.

The Christmas party was already in full swing and the sound of Bing Crosby could barely be heard over the loud jovial sounds of the party. Tree branches dipped from the high ceiling, and were entwined with silver bells and mistletoe, forming clusters and tunnels. The heavy smell of pine needles tickled Irene's nose.

Two bars were on opposite sides of the crowded space. There was a huge punch bowl filled with champagne and raspberry sherbet. Along the far wall, a long buffet table was heaped with cold and hot appetizers: mounds of shrimp, cheeses of all sizes and shapes, crudités, stuffed mushrooms, and a decorated platter of sliced meats.

Kevin's eyes narrowed as he took in the enormous, overly decorated room. He couldn't help but compare this event to the annual Christmas party at his own office which was carefully orchestrated not to be wasteful. There, conversations remained respectful, and drinking kept to a minimum, but Kevin knew the restrained atmosphere changed as soon as he said his good-byes and left, handing each of his employees an envelope containing their bonuses.

Irene leaned in toward Kevin, "This is so, so over the top."

"I warned you." He withdrew an envelope, and handed his coat to the butler, saying to Irene, "I'll be right with you."

Shouldering her way past groups of merry-makers, she heard bits and pieces of conversation, some back-slapping, and the high pitch of female laughter. Six young women squeezed together to take a selfie. A waiter sidled up to her, one hand offering a tray of meatballs while the other held paper napkins. She declined saying, "No thanks."

Threading her way to one of the bars, Irene requested a glass of white wine and stood to the side, staring at the crowd of guests eating and drinking and laughing. The overburdened buffet table turned her stomach. She covered her mouth to the sour tang of waste.

She took a step back and thought of the many hungry mouths this party could feed. A feeling of helplessness came over her in waves. It was the same frustration she felt each Christmas morning while serving the hungry at her uncle's bar, and at the soup kitchen, knowing she could never fill the children's hunger. And then a gut-wrenching guilt would overcome her while driving to the Golf Club, where she had to perform her wifely duties amongst the plentitude of wealth. The recall never failed to leave a bitter taste in her mouth. A lump formed in the back of her throat.

She put her glass aside on the bar. Sounding like an attack of bees circling her head, raucous laughter burst from all sides. The limbs of the overburdened Christmas tree were drooping with the weight of ornaments, branches of holly dripping with red berries, pressed down on her head, dwarfing her very height.

Eyes sweeping the room, she looked for Kevin, but she couldn't spot him.

She felt a tap her on the shoulder.

"Having fun, darling?"

As though a rock had been hurled at her stomach, she stifled a scream. "Ashford!"

CHAPTER FIFTY-SIX

A sarcastic grin was painted on Ashford's face, his chest puffed up in superiority. In the depth of his eyes, Irene saw bottomless pits of fury. The very sound of his commanding voice caused her body to clench, starting with her jaw and ending at her toes.

"I'd quite forgotten to send you the invitation. Yet here you are." His eyes traveled from her head to her breasts, her hips, and back again to her face. "Nothing has changed. You're still a lump of clay."

Fingers curled into fists, "Have you signed the papers?"

"What papers would that be?"

"The separation agreements."

"What? I can't hear you."

Gritting her teeth, she knew he was egging her on. Her throat tightened. She would not let him bring her down to his level. "My attorney is waiting for your signature."

Irene felt as though she was sitting on her own shoulder, talking to herself, reinforcing herself, strengthening her own decisions and resolve. She took a deep breath. Stepping right up close to Ashford, she said, "You can't belittle me anymore. You can't taunt and criticize me anymore. I can't be molded by you or anyone else. I own myself."

With a sharp movement, she turned and bumped directly into Kevin.

"I was just coming to find you." Placing his hand on her shoulder, he asked "Are you all right? You seemed distraught."

"I'm fine." A smile reduced the wrinkles on her forehead and turned the corners of her lips upward. "Actually, I'm better than ever."

Kevin indicated his head toward Ashford. "Did you know he's the president of the condo board here? And I assume he's responsible for this extravagance. Actually," he turned to Ashford, "I have a question for you. Did you take a vote, or just deplete the budget on your own accord?" He leaned in closer, and whispered, "Padding the expenses? Kickbacks? Is that your game?"

Ashford's eyes narrowed to slits. His lips formed a tight line, the cords of his neck strained at his collar. "Don't you accuse me."

Irene looked at the two men locked in a duel.

"Ashford, just sign the papers."

"Never!"

Standing firm, Irene did not shrink back. She would not be diminished. "Ashford, I know you don't want to go to court. Just sign the papers."

Kevin, his arm resting on Irene's shoulder, lifted his chin. "If I were you, I'd do as she asks."

"But I'm not you, asshole. She knows what I'm capable of."

Irene shrugged off Kevin's arm and moved close to Ashford. Her eyes shined as though in a dare. Adrenaline rushed through her body. She felt an itch, an unfamiliar urge to whack him. She folded her arms across her chest. "And you don't know what I'm capable of."

CHAPTER FIFTY-SEVEN

Tourists who browse Fifth Avenue stop at Rockefeller Center and stand in awe of the magnificent Christmas tree overlooking the skating rink. Truly a crowd-pleaser, the giant tree, usually a Norway Spruce, is almost ninety feet tall and will stay lit until just after New Year's Day.

Irene and Julia, arms linked, skated with ease on the rink's outer perimeter, their movements graceful and in synch. In the middle of the ice rink, a single skater dressed in red drew Julia's attention with her dance moves. Withdrawing her arm, Julia twirled once, and skated backward, facing Irene. "She could be a champion."

"That girl likes attention."

"Doesn't everyone?"

Irene shook her head. "Not me."

They skated one by one to avoid the hundred and fifty other skaters on the ice, some proficient, others struggling to keep upright.

Julia nudged Irene as they circled the rink. "You're so quiet these days. What's gotten into you?"

"Not much going on, just really tired."

"Playing every night?"

"Some afternoons, too. Lessons."

"Oh, it's so difficult to get my students to concentrate. I don't know what they think about, but it certainly is not their flute lessons."

"They may get inspired sometime in the future. I have three girls who come together for their piano lessons. They would stay at the piano all day and night if they could. It's their treat for good behavior."

Irene slowed, skated on one skate to make a quick circle, then linked arms with Julia again. "The girls come from the projects. I wish I could help them more than the couple of hours a week."

Irene took off her mittens, pulled a tissue from her pocket, and wiped her dripping nose. "I wanted nothing more than skating lessons when I was a little kid." She remembered dreaming of being a ballerina on ice, wearing a skater's sequined dress, tying the laces of bright white skates.

Floating over the blue frozen water, her dream ended with her father yelling. "You're a good for nothing. One big fat zero."

Ashford was just like that, shaming her, belittling her every move. Irene shook her head at the parallel. The verbal attacks were as harmful as if they had been physical assaults. Did denigrating a daughter or a wife serve to increase the stature of a husband or father? Did it fuel their ego, brand them as masculine and important, or simply ensure they had the power and control?

Irene did a snow-plow stop, steadied herself, and began to glide, thinking of better days, a time in her teens when she skated on the frozen fish pond in the park. She loved the fresh clear air, the freedom of movement. She'd learned some trick turns from the older girls, and would stay out long after dark. Her uncle was not too happy about that. He'd take her cold hands between his and warm them, saying she shouldn't spend so much time on anything frivolous, but should concentrate her skills on the piano.

Julia interrupted Irene's thoughts. "Mind if we take a break? My feet are frozen solid."

"Me too. I've had enough for the day."

The rental skates returned, the women went into a restaurant by the rink for a late lunch, each ordering a bloody Mary. Irene gave the menu a quick look, and then closed it. Julia deliberated over the menu, her forefinger pressed to her lips, her eyes shifting over the possibilities. She pointed to the Reuben sandwich, shifted in her seat, and said to the waiter, "I'll have what she's having: rabbit food with a bit of protein."

"Ma'am?"

Julia sighed as though she'd never had a real choice. "We'll both have a chef salad."

Though the café was crowded, they were seated at a small table for two facing the golden sculpture of Prometheus, the Greek god.

Irene placed the linen napkin on her lap. "Look at that devious Titan molding men from clay. He was a crafty son-of-a-bitch."

"At least he got what he deserved as punishment."

Irene shook her head, her hands pulled at the napkin. "Crafty and deceitful, just like someone I know."

"Oh no. Ashford's being Ashford?"

"Keeps saying he'll sign, but hasn't actually done it."

"Is that why you're so quiet these days?"

"That, and a problem I can't seem to get straight in my mind."

"Does it have to do with Kevin?"

"No. It's kind of a moral, or maybe ethical, conundrum."

"So? Out with it."

Irene, nibbling on her lower lip, closed her eyes, took a deep breath, and leaned forward. "Okay, it's like this. You know we lived a really high life style. The cash I've been living on these past months is the money that I siphoned off each week from the household budget that Ashford gave me. He never for one moment missed that amount I squirreled away. I did it for years. I don't mean to make it sound easy." She looked at the ceiling. "It was really deceptive of me."

Julia reached across the table. "After all he put you through, you shouldn't for one moment feel bad."

"That's not it. The cash sitting in my safety deposit box came from…" she pulled her lips to a tight line before she could continue. "Look, I always thought Ashford earned a high income, a lot of money, and since I did what was required of me as his wife, I thought it was reasonable to keep a portion for myself. In my own way, I was securing my future."

"I don't see your problem. When he signs the divorce, you'll have plenty of money, so don't worry about that little bit."

"Stop." She lifted her hand, palm forward. "Ashford's clients had fraudulently been depleted of their trusts. He cheated his clients. So, all that money that sits in my safety deposit box belongs to someone else, and I don't know what I'm supposed to do with it."

"My two cents: enjoy it."

"Don't you understand? It's stolen money."

"Okay, I get it. Ashford's a snake."

A strained silence hung across the table. Irene roped the napkin around her fingers and clasped her knees together. Julia, fidgeting in her seat, offered a fake smile, and finally said, "I mean, he is a lawyer, right? Certainly he earned a portion of the income."

"I'm sure he worked for part of it, but the rest? I keep wrestling with this. Should I keep it, or give part of it to charity? What charity? What portion? I haven't a clue what to do."

Julia placed her hands flat on the table. "Don't do anything."

The waiter placed their drinks on the table. Celery stalks jutted from the goblets. Irene's hand shook as she lifted the glass to her lips, tomato juice spilling over the edge, soiling the white linen table cloth.

"Oh, you are a mess." Julia patted the tablecloth. "I don't mean the spilled drink. You're driving yourself bonkers. Take my advice and stop worrying about it." Her eyes wide open, she said, "Listen to me. Don't do anything. Just use that money for yourself."

"Of course, that's an option. It's just making me more than uneasy. It's a real dilemma."

"One thing's for sure: you're not thinking of giving any of it back to the bastard. He stole it. Not you. You can threaten him with disclosing the fraud. For Christ's sake, he's an attorney. He knows what will happen if you—"

"I signed a confidentiality agreement."

"You what?"

"He demanded I sign that document before he would sign the divorce agreement. And I did."

"And your lawyer let you?"

Irene nodded, took a long sigh, tears pooling in her moist eyes. "I'm cornered. I don't know what's right. Who does that money belong to?"

CHAPTER FIFTY-EIGHT

At the insistent ring of his cell, Kevin pushed the delete button, and turned his full attention back to Walter, his assistant. "Are you certain?"

"Absolutely. The invoices from the caterer don't add up to anything close to legitimate."

"Cleaning service?"

"That, too."

Nodding, Kevin drummed his fingers on the desk. "Let me take a look at the figures for the past six months. And bring me the governing documents for that building."

The assistant stood, tightening the Windsor knot of his tie. "Gloria's been trying to reach you. She's called a few times already. I told her you were in conference. She's insistent, for sure." He indicated the cell sitting at the edge of the desk, then gathered his notes, nodded, and left, closing the door behind himself.

Kevin sat back in his desk chair, and swivelled to face the window. It had been a seasonably cold December. Long icicles formed like spears from the roofs of the buildings across the avenue. They were like the huge dripping stalactites he'd seen in the Luray Caverns, when his mother had dragged him from school on a last-minute trip to Virginia. During the bumpy train ride she had barely spoken to him, but stared through the streaked window at the passing run-down cottages scattered here and there along the rails. She seemed lost in thoughts of her own. But as they wandered the caves, she held his hand in a tight grip, imploring him to stay close and never leave. Until that moment he'd thought his mother was unshakeable, self-confident, but when he'd looked up, he saw her smile tight and brows pulled together. Written on her face was fear.

The cell's ring tone broke the silence. He threw his hands in the air and, with a frown, pulled the phone to him and answered Gloria's call.

"I'm moving back to California." Her husky voice cracked. "And Nick's coming with me."

Kevin sat up straight in his chair. "Slow down. What are you talking about?"

"Exactly what I said."

"I had no idea you were thinking this. Shouldn't we discuss a sudden move like this?"

"Mind's made up." She was just like his mother

Kevin could almost visualize her face: rigid jaw set and eyes narrowed. She would be taking frequent small breaths, her pretense needing oxygen. He wondered if he should coddle her, make it easy for her, or just say a quick good-bye.

He shook his head, knowing this was not his way. "Okay, Gloria. What do you want me to do?"

"Kevin, you were my first love." The seductive voice deepened and oozed like milk chocolate in the hot sun. "From the moment I saw you working on the crossword puzzle with a fountain pen, I knew, no matter what, you were to be my lifelong love. Remember that first moment?"

"Yes, I haven't forgotten"

"It was of our future."

He paused, recalling an image of the Gloria in their youth. Slowly, that picture began to wrinkle and shrivel, and the façade of today's Gloria came into focus: the dyed hair, the injections, the face lifts, the nude photos.

"You've been so good to me."

"I'm listening." He closed his eyes, wondering what drama was about to unfold.

"I couldn't have found a better man than you."

"You tried how many times? Four marriages? Or is there a fifth I don't know about?"

"You could be the fifth if you wanted to marry me again."

Kevin sloughed off her comment as a delaying technique. "Why don't you, just for a change, say what you want."

"It's money."

"Of course, it always involves money."

"A lot of—"

"How much?"

"You're good at numbers and figures. How much would the rent be for the condo I'm living in, I mean, for the rest of my life?"

He laughed aloud, and stroked the little scar above his eye. "That depends on how long you intend to live."

"A long, very long time."

"That's a good attitude."

"Thank you."

"Look, Gloria, stop all this calculating. I'll help you out as I have before, but there is one proviso. I insist you don't force Nick to live with you on the west coast. Let Nick make his own decision."

"Don't you think it's a little late in the game to play daddy?"

The undertone of sarcasm was not lost on Kevin, who was quick to retort, "It's never too late."

"Agreed."

"We'll talk to Nick together."

"Why don't you give me a good-bye party? I'll invite all my new friends, and you can entertain us with your guitar. Oh, and sweetheart, I have one little tiny request." Her voice purred, and Kevin could envision the swivel of her hips, the smile on her lips, and the tilt of her head when she wanted something. "I would really and truly love the painting in your living room to bring with me to my new apartment. You know, the one of the man and horse. It will remind me of our days together."

Kevin squinted, and closed his eyes. "Gloria, you never know when enough is enough."

CHAPTER FIFTY-NINE

"Every moment of every day you have choices; some little, some big."
Kevin leaned across the sticky plastic table. "Very few decisions are
forever. But this one is. This one is life-changing."

Nick brought the cup of steaming coffee to his mouth and blew across
the top. His eyes skipped from the dirty window reflecting both his father
and himself to the depth of the trembling coffee. He slumped over the
table. "I tried to walk it off, but it won't leave me alone or go away. I
walked all day, but nothing helped."

"You did the right thing by calling me."

Nick's hands were clenched into fists. His damp shirt clung to his
body. Sweat prickled his groin. Temptation stood just on the other side of
the wide congested avenue. It was dark on the streets, the days short and
the nights long. It was dark inside Nick. The animal's bite dug deep.
Drugs stood just on the other side of the congested avenue. To cross
against the light was suicide. The itch continued.

"Every day, you must chose to go right or go left."

"You don't know what it's like. It's an animal gnawing inside of me."

"But you haven't given in to the temptation."

"I'm close."

"You're strong. You called for help."

He snorted. "You know nothing about me."

Kevin paused, his eyes clouding with tears. "Look at me."

Nick obeyed, his head cocked to the side. "What?"

"This is what I know about you. You are my son. Everything about you
is of Gloria and me. We have some good and bad qualities, some strengths
and some weaknesses. Please, Nick, get the professional help you need." He
rubbed his forehead until his fingertips left the little scar above his eye red and
raw. "All we did together was give you life, and life is never a sure thing."

"So I've heard."

"It's not all about your genetics, but also the culture and values you
were exposed to, and the people you chose to be with, the things you

determined to do. That's what makes you you. And I love you." He looked down at his empty palms. "Honestly, I'm not making excuses for myself, but you know there were obstacles. And the few days I spent with you every year were never enough, but I tried my best."

Nick pushed the coffee cup away.

"So all I ask of you is to try your best. It's what you do with the time you have that's important. Don't blow it on a quick fix. That never lasts."

"I know."

"You don't have to be alone in this."

"Yeah? Do you see Riley sitting here with me? She helped me. We were together, climbing out of the pit." Nick slumped further down in the seat. "And I left her in that rat hole of a hotel room." His voice shook. He banged the heel of his hand on his forehead. "She was in such bad shape. I'll never forgive myself."

"Nick, don't beat yourself up over her. She was a user, a user of people and drugs. You have to move forward."

"It's too hard alone."

Kevin sat back against the ripped vinyl of the booth, the edges prodding his shoulder blade. He took a deep breath, and watched his son double over in agony. Kevin stifled a sob, wanting to help his son, but not knowing how. He had let twenty years slip by expecting the kid to grow up, be healthy, and lead a good life.

Kevin rubbed his eyes, and caught the reflection of Nick and himself sitting across from each other in a diner. Skidding into his mind was his own father, a man he never knew, a man who was only a photograph sitting in a frame, a man who died as a war hero. Alone, his mother had filled the empty spaces of a father. Gloria had filled the role of father with an assortment of men.

Pressing forward, he grasped Nick's arm and held it in a vise. "You are not alone. I'm here with you. You can always count on me."

"Don't you understand? I left her."

"Yes, and you saved yourself."

CHAPTER SIXTY

Irene sat on the edge of the hotel bed, her cell phone gripped in her hand. Answering on the fourth tone, she bit down on her lower lip as Ashford's voice thundered through the connection.

"You lousy, lice-infected piece of shit. You'll never get a penny, not one god-damned red cent. You'll live in a sewer for the rest of your meaningless life. Rats will eat better than you. I'll bring you down, you worthless blob of rubbish."

The phone dangled from her hand while Ashford kept on with his verbal abuse. She looked down at her bare feet, and wondered how long the tirade would continue until he said what he called about.

"Are you there?" He shouted. "Don't you dare put down the phone. You're in this mess as deep as me. Answer me."

"What mess?"

"As if you didn't know! You've no way to wiggle your fat ass out. You signed."

"The confidentiality? Of course, you saw me sign."

"Not that! The tax returns."

Wrinkles at the corner of her eyes deepened. "The tax returns?"

"You stupid bitch. You reported me."

She heard panic in his voice as it rose to a higher pitch.

"I don't know what you're talking about. I've done no such thing."

"An I.R.S. audit of five years, you should rot in hell."

Irene heard the call end with the sound of the dial tone. She looked across the spare room at the mute television. She wished Ashford had one of those buttons she could hit and then never have to hear his voice ever again. Why had she continued to listen to his barrage of venom? Whatever he had done with the returns and his finances were strictly his doing. He might get caught in a tangle of fraud and lies, but she had not been the cause of his problem. She had not even been party to his misdeeds. It did seem curious, though, that the I.R.S. would delve into his tax returns just at this time. One way or another, she hoped he'd get his comeuppance.

She sat for a moment, shaking her head in disbelief at never having dared to argue with Ashford. Not then and not now. Why couldn't she stop the onslaught? With her father, she had never dared to quarrel, much less disagree. Neither had her mother had the strength or will to put an end to the abuse. With a chill, Irene remembered her mother jammed in the corner of the living room, the shabby armchair blocking her, her father's arm raised as the filth of his words flew with spit from his mouth. Irene's small hands tugged at his waist. She'd been plucked aside like a mere piece of lint.

Irene jumped up from the bed and tripped on her way to the closet, blaming herself for allowing the abuse to continue. Just like her mother, she had permitted herself to be abused for years. She grabbed her heavy coat, closed and locked the door, and stormed to the elevator. Never, never again, she vowed.

The icy weather whipped at her as soon as she pushed through the revolving door. Not wanting to be late to meet Julia, she hurried along the slippery streets. The day before had brought heavy snows to the city, and though the sidewalks had been shoveled and the streets plowed, patches of thin ice remained, and huge puddles of dirty water had collected at the corners.

Irene moved along quickly, and reached Julia waiting for her inside the lobby of Kevin's building. Her nose red and dripping, her shoes water-logged, she gave their names to the concierge who told them to take the elevator to the seventh floor.

"I could barely wait until today." Julia blew on her hands. "Winters kill me. All I get is sleet and ice and dreams of sunshine. I'm cold until April."

"Same here." Irene stuffed her gloves into the pocket of her coat, untied her woolen scarf, and stretched and clenched her fingers. "Got to get the blood moving, I'm frozen."

The warmth and quiet of the private elevator held both women within their own thoughts 'til the door slid open on the marble foyer where Kevin stood, wearing a dark turtle neck sweater and jeans. He hugged both women, and ushered them into the apartment.

"Welcome. How 'bout a cup of coffee first?"

Julia's eyes were wide. "How 'bout a tour first?"

Though Irene was accustomed to wealth, she was impressed by the overall tone of Kevin's apartment. where the chairs in the dining room were aligned, the table tops were clutter free, and the up-to-date kitchen spotless. But what most caught her eye was the living room, with the grand piano beckoning to her. She couldn't help but think of her three students coming from the projects, and the limitations they faced and how they loved the touch of the ivory keys under their fingers, their delight at playing the piano infectious; the one hour a week filled with laughter and serious effort. For Irene, it was the bright spot in her days. Last week, she gave each of the girls' families a turkey as a Christmas gift, wishing she could do more for them. She wondered if she'd be financially able to do that again.

The three drank their coffee in the kitchen sitting on the barstools, Irene eyeing the piano. "Mind if I get right to it?"

"It's there waiting for you."

With a bold stride, Irene went to the piano, trailed one finger over the ivories, and sat down. Looking back at Kevin and Julia, she nodded, lifted her hands in parody of a concert pianist, and dove in to the keyboard with a jazz rendition of "Chopsticks." Kevin slid onto the bench and joined in playing on the upper register.

He was so close, she could feel heat roar through her body. The scent of his after-shave lingered in the air and bathed her. Her heart sprinted, and she wondered if he could feel it reaching toward him. She couldn't help but laugh aloud, and played an arpeggio up and down the keyboard, leaning close to Kevin. His hands joined hers, their arms entangled.

"Okay, you two. That's enough tomfoolery." Julia took her flute from the case. "We need this rehearsal. At least I need it. Maybe you two are all set, but I'm not. And no interruptions. No ringing phones. Put your cells on silent."

Kevin looked at Irene, stopped laughing, stroked her forearm, and lingered a moment before getting up from the piano and picking up his guitar. He placed his phone on mute, and stood to the side of the piano.

It took several trials and missteps before the trio found their groove. They worked on transitions from the classical form of Kevin's composition to improvisational jazz. Throughout the morning they worked, stopping at times to complement each other, or make suggestions. They alternated solo sections, and by early afternoon, they were satisfied with the results.

Julia wiped her flute dry. "That's it for me. I think we sound great." She looked at Irene, a twinkling in her eye. "I've got to go. An early lesson."

"Let me take you both to lunch." The guitar dangled from Kevin's hand.

"No, you two go and enjoy. The last thing I need is to be late for this lesson. The parents would never forgive me if I let their precious daughter wait one extra minute. The sun rises and sets on this one. If only the kid had talent…"

Irene remained on the piano bench while Kevin escorted Julia to the elevator. Her fingers danced lightly over the keys with the tingle of expectation, until Kevin returned and sat close to her on the piano bench.

"We can bundle up and go out for lunch, or stay here warm and cozy."

She could feel his breath on her cheeks. The nearness of his body set her aglow. "Are you asking for my vote?"

He nodded.

The hummingbirds fluttered in her stomach. She wanted to kiss his mouth, caress his face, nuzzle his neck. Her voice cracked as the words tumbled from her mouth. "If you have eggs…"

"We'll stay here." He leaned in toward her, and placed his warm hands on either side of her face, drawing her closer until their lips met.

The kiss lasted a lifetime, his lips gentle and warm until an urgency filled them both and they were locked together. When they finally drew apart, Irene's lips were tender, her body was breathless with longing. Irene knew that from this moment on, her life would be forever altered. "I've never been kissed like that before."

"There is no 'before,' only 'now' is important." His lips sought hers, their bodies pressed tight together again, until Irene drew back for a breath, and then pressed her cheek against his chest.

Kevin placed a palm on her forehead, stroked the hair back from her face with the gentlest of touches, and murmured in her ear, "I see such goodness in you."

Enfolded in his arms, her eyes closed, she sank into his low voice and gentle hands. She heard his stomach rumble, and a giggle escaped her throat.

Kevin coughed, covering the sound. He tilted her radiant face and kissed her long neck, cupped her chin, and ran his tongue over her eyelids.

Irene sank into a moment that felt so natural, and yet so unexpected and foreign. She felt she had entered a state of other-worldliness. She savored this moment and never wanted to leave his embrace.

He murmured again, "Tell me all about yourself. I want to know everything about you."

"Not much to tell."

"How did you grow to be this wonderful woman."

She didn't want to spoil the moment by telling him of the chilling fear that permeated the house of her childhood, the lack of a mother's love, or of her abusive father, and the fire that had led to her uncle, and the empty years with Ashford. Her life had been a long and difficult journey to this moment. Held in his arms, Irene felt she deserved this happiness.

She sighed, and spoke against his chest. "The piano saved me from a lonely life."

"Did you always want to be a pianist? Even as a youngster?"

Startled by the sound of high heels pounding across the entry, Kevin jerked back. "Could only be my ex, Gloria."

Irene sprang upright as Gloria burst from the foyer, shouting and sobbing, "He's gone!" she screamed and collapsed on the carpet. "Nick's gone!"

CHAPTER SIXTY-ONE

Sprawled on the Persian rug, Gloria howled, "Nick's gone."

Kevin lurched from the piano bench, and grasped Gloria's shoulders in a firm grip. "What do you mean Nick's gone?'"

"He's emptied my medicine chest and—"

"When did he go?"

"I don't know."

"Think, Gloria. How long ago."

She shook her head, sputtering, "I don't know when—"

"What pills did he take?"

"All of them."

Irene slipped off the piano bench and moved toward the window.

Gloria's eyes were flooded with tears, and mascara ran in rivulets down her cheeks. Her eyes travelled around the room, then narrowed on Irene. In a flash, the emerald eyes shifted and hardened from anguish to bitterness. The tears stopped as though on command. "Who's she?"

"A friend of mine." Kevin's voice was muted.

Gloria's eyebrows raised. "A friend? Why is she here?"

Kevin swallowed. "Irene is a close friend"

In a soft voice, Irene said, "Yes, I'm a close friend."

Gloria's eyes then flickered back to Kevin. She raised her shoulders as though in innocence. "Everything. Nick took everything!" She tucked her knees under herself, her skirt slipped up to reveal her upper thighs and red panties.

Irene steadied herself, clasping her fingertips on the window ledge. She could only imagine the worst possible feeling, that of a parent losing a child.

Gloria's voice screamed, "All my jewelry! He took it all."

"What the hell happened? He was doing so well."

"He was."

"Did anything else happen?"

"I told him to start packing"

"His clothes?"

"I wanted him to come with me to California."

"Didn't you tell him he could stay here? Gloria, we agreed he would make his own decision, that we wouldn't force anything on him. God, Gloria. He was doing so well. What did you do?"

The age lines deepened around her mouth and eyes. "Don't blame this on me. I didn't cause him to go off the deep end."

"Well, what the hell happened?"

She thrust her hands out, palms up. "Riley called."

Kevin bent over, and sank down on the couch, his elbows on his knees, his head held in his hands. In the slump of his shoulders, Irene could see the impact of his loss, the worst possible occurrence in a father's life. Wanting to comfort him, hold him in her arms, kiss his lips and the scar on his forehead, Irene felt the pain and burden he must bear, the loss of his son to drugs.

Not saying anything, she moved into the kitchen, searched until she found the makings of tea, steeped the leaves in a glass teapot, and poured steaming tea into two mugs. She placed them on the table in front of the couch with a dish of sliced lemon and sugar.

Kevin looked up, nodded a thank you, and picked up the mug with both hands. His focus shifted to the ceiling, and then to Irene. Written all over his body was the devastating news of his child's fall back into the world of drugs, the dreams and hopes of a parent smashed.

"After his second time in rehab, it was like a rebirth. I had such hopes for him."

Irene placed a palm on his shoulder, and leaned down close to him. "I know." He caressed the back of her hand with his sturdy fingertips.

Gloria grasped Kevin's forearm. "My gorgeous emerald necklace. Gone! You know, the one that was your mother's."

"I should go,"

Overpowered by Gloria's insistent pull, Kevin's attention shifted to her.

"Is that what you're worried about, your jewelry? Not your son? Not the devastation? Not the life he's sunk back into? Damn it, I thought he was strong!"

Gloria grumbled, "Not strong enough for Riley. She probably put on the emerald earrings as soon as Nick opened his hand, gobbled down pills, and sold my diamond. I wouldn't trust that piece of shit as far as I could throw her."

Kevin turned away from Gloria and looked up at Irene with such hurt in his eyes that Irene felt tears gather and drip from her lower lid. She wiped her cheek, wondering how this charming, talented, caring man had married such a manipulative drama queen. "I don't know what to say. I'm so sorry."

He shook his head. "I thought I'd learned to expect the unexpected. I didn't see this coming. I just don't know how that Riley could wind him around her finger like that."

Flipping off her spike heels, Gloria pulled at her short skirt and stood. "You'd have to have seen her in action to get the real picture. Wiggles her hips and takes off her clothes at the slightest… I always knew that girl was trouble. Didn't I tell you that? First time I laid eyes on her, I could see what she was all about. A gold digger from the start."

Kevin rubbed the scar on his forehead until it was red and bruised. "Talking like that, Gloria, doesn't help one little bit. So cut it out."

"Don't talk to me like that. I'm his mother. You never took the slightest bit of interest. And now, here under your roof, you wanted to play daddy, and look where it got you."

Irene took a step back. "I think I should go. If I can help in any way…" It was just something to say. She knew she had no way of helping, but neither parent was thinking straight. Kevin blamed himself, and Gloria blamed Riley.

How quickly things can change. In one moment, Kevin's dreams and wishes for his son had been punctured, his hopes that this time would be different, and his son would be whole, dashed. She wondered if Kevin had been realistic.

The heels of her sturdy loafers scuffed along the marble floor. She lingered in the foyer. The loving moments of Kevin's arms encircling her lingered with each breath she took. The warmth of his touch remained on her lips. Just a few moments ago, her body had tingled under his touch, and she wanted to stay in his arms for the rest of her life, share all the hours of every day. With Kevin by her side, life would take on a deeper meaning. They would be good for each other.

She didn't know if her heart was breaking or aching for Kevin. Words of comfort had stuck in her throat. Should she leave, or should she stay?

Her shoulders drooped, and she wiped her nose. The crystal chandelier lowered on her. Palms pressed hard against her head, she leaned against the wall. Nothing she did seemed right. How she wanted to be a caring person for Kevin. This was his time of need, and she stood in his foyer, her feet stuck on the floor, unable to help.

Breezing past Irene, Gloria bustled across the marble floor, her spike heels clattering on the hard stone. Without acknowledging Irene, she stomped her way out of the apartment, her fur coat trailing behind her.

Unable to go forward, Irene stood watching the doors of the elevator close behind Gloria.

CHAPTER SIXTY-TWO

Irene stayed in the hall, listening to the somber sounds of sadness coming from the tones of Kevin's guitar. Eventually, she walked toward the living room. Her heavy steps were filled with sorrow. In the dim light of the late afternoon, she could see a shadow, an outline of Kevin sitting on the sofa, his head to the side as he strummed minor chords.

"You coming back for more? Haven't you done enough?"

Struck, Irene took a step back. She heard no rage in his voice, but despair. She stepped forward. She saw his long fingers loosen on the frets. "Kevin. It's me, Irene. Do you want me to leave?"

In one swift movement, he put the guitar on the coffee table, got up from the couch, and opened his arms, welcoming her. He enfolded her in an embrace of heartache. "No, no, no, of course I don't want you to leave. I thought it was Gloria coming back."

She could feel strength in his broad chest and strong arms, yet she also felt his despair in the curve of his neck as he took a deep breath. Without saying a word to one another, they stood holding onto each other, their bodies delivering messages of caring and hope, and maybe a glimmer of love.

Reluctant to separate, they did draw apart, but Irene kept her arm around his waist, smiling up into his moist eyes. They took thoughtful steps as he led her back to the couch. Irene curled in his arms, not wanting to leave his side.

He rubbed the tip of her nose with his. "I'm glad you came back. Otherwise I'd have had to go out into the cold night searching for you at that awful hotel lounge."

"I'm only playing three nights a week now, and tonight's not one of those."

"Good timing for us."

Her thoughts scrambled, she pressed a hand on his chest. "Do you want to talk about Nick?"

She felt his body tense and hesitate.

"It's just so hard to imagine he's put himself back in hell. God only knows where he'll end up. Knowing Gloria, I've not heard the whole story. If only she'd left Nick alone, but no, she had to butt in again, hurting everyone, wanting more and more. She's a menace. I'm certain something else happened."

He shook his head as though to rid himself of negative thoughts. "The kid was riddled with guilt. He left Riley overdosing in some cheap hotel. But he was strong, didn't succumb to any sort of drugs. Even after he injured his ankle, he wouldn't take anything. Not even an aspirin. He was really doing so well. And he was so proud of himself. And I was very proud of him."

His arm around Irene's shoulder felt heavy. She wanted to lighten his sorrow, but couldn't find the words that would help. She lifted her face, her velvet eyes filled with understanding. "I hope he'll be alright."

With his palm, he smoothed the hair back from her forehead. He took her hand and held the palm to his mouth, then kissed her fingers, one at a time.

Heaving a huge breath, he said, "Let's not talk about Nick."

"Sometimes it's good to talk, not keep everything bottled up inside. Maybe I can help…"

"You have your own problems."

She chuckled, "Doesn't everyone?"

"You're a good soul. Ashford's a damn fool."

Comfortable in Kevin's arms, Irene sensed the inevitable. They would go to bed. She had felt his arousal. Maybe tonight, though she thought the upset of Nick may have removed any such thought of romance. Feeling his body heat through her blouse, she couldn't help but feel her body and its growing warmth. Her eyes closed in wanting. She slid off her loafers and let them drop to the floor.

There was a stalled sense in the predictable. She dangled her foot over the edge of the couch. It wasn't quite impatience she felt. Rather, it was a building tension, like waiting for the second hand on a repaired clock to strike midnight, marking the end of a year and beginning of another.

She placed her cheek on his chest, and felt it rising and falling in an increased rhythm. What was he waiting for? She stirred, sat up, and reached for his hand. He would be tender and thoughtful. He would undress her. His long fingers would glide over her flesh. She would hold the fire at her core until he was inside her.

He bent down toward her lips. The light kiss lingered, then filled them both as their bodies clung tightly to each other. When they drew apart, he said, a smile tilting the corners of his wet lip, "I haven't felt that in a long time."

Staring into his eyes, she placed his hand on her breast and said, "Shall we?"

An exchanged smile, and they walked a slow lingering pace to the bedroom while, button by button, Kevin removed her blouse, slid her skirt down, and unhooked her bra. Lastly, he glided her lace thong down to her ankles. His hands on her hips, he kissed her belly, her breasts, and neck, and lips, and murmured, "You're so beautiful."

Trembling with want and desire, Irene unbuckled his belt, unzipped his slacks, and slipped down his jockey shorts.

He cleared his throat. "Are you sure about this?"

"A little late to ask."

CHAPTER SIXTY-THREE

A feeling of renewal came over Irene. Being with Kevin every possible moment for the past several weeks, only leaving each other's side to carry on daily responsibilities, Kevin remained uppermost on her mind, even while sitting at the piano playing for the late dinner crowd or teaching her students an easy Bach piece. There he was, a film playing before her eyes, caressing and holding her close, saying he loved her.

During the years of marriage to Ashford, Irene had felt she deserved nothing better than living as an empty shell. She'd read books, seen films, talked to other women, and knew that life could be fulfilling. Often bitter with her hollow life, the piano had been her refuge. Ashford had no knowledge of how much music meant to her, as Irene made certain to play only when he was not in the house. Though music filled her empty heart, it hadn't been enough.

The past weeks, while crocuses peeked through the earth and snow flurries danced outside the windows, Irene played Kevin's baby grand with abandon, discovering the freedom to improvise, to create. And with that feeling of liberty, she found her heart enlarge with enough room to love fully and completely, greeting each day with energy and spirit, and love of another.

Waking alone in her hotel bed, Irene snuggled the pillows as though they were Kevin's warm body. Reliving his tenderness, she was lost in the pleasurable memory of his fingers roaming her flesh, his lips upon her thighs, his tongue seeking her wet lips. They reached intimate knowledge of each other's sexual wants, attaining exquisite moments.

Cuddling her pillow, Irene whispered into the empty hotel room, "I love you, Kevin." Then she said it out loud, liking the way it sounded, "I love you."

Startled by the ring tone of her phone, Irene thrust off her bed covers and grabbed for her cell. Anticipating the sound of Kevin's voice, she flopped down on the edge of the bed when she heard the voice of her attorney.

"Irene, good morning. I hope I haven't awakened you."

"Not at all." She envisioned his full head of snow white hair, and the blue veins on his spotted hands.

"I wanted to tell you before it reached the newspapers."

Irene's back straightened, and she dug her toes into the thin carpet. Everything had been going so well over the past months, she knew her ivory tower was about to fall. "Oh my God, is this bad news?"

"Only for Ashford. He's looking at a prison term of five years."

"What? How?"

"He's been indicted for conspiracy to defraud the United States, corruptly endeavoring to impede the internal revenue laws, and tax evasion."

"You mean the IRS? He cheated on his tax returns. He signed my name." Her brows drew together, and she gasped. "You saw that wasn't my signature."

"Rest easy, Irene. There's proof the signature is a forgery. Further, you will not be held responsible for your husband's schemes."

"I don't know what all this means." Her hand flew to her bare neck as her mind filled with questions. Was she supposed to do something? How was she supposed to feel? Thoughts whizzed through her mind and froze as the attorney continued.

"Your husband filed fraudulent personal, corporate, and charitable trust returns, and then made false statements during the audit of a phony charity he had set up and used to steal more than four million dollars."

Irene's eyes opened wide as dollar signs galloped across the room. "That's how he purchased the house? That's how we lived the way we did, the wealthy lifestyle? The Country Club? The Manhattan apartment? I was the dumb participant. I don't know what I'm supposed to do."

"This is your attorney speaking. You are to do nothing."

"He'll lose his license and practice."

"That's the least of it. He faces five years on the tax evasion charge and another three years for obstruction. Understand, these are accusations, and your husband is presumed innocent until proven guilty."

Irene closed her eyes as the reality of her lawyer's words began to penetrate. "He's guilty. I know it."

"If convicted, the sentencing will be determined by the judge."

Irene was finding it difficult to swallow, and her voice sounded more like a croak. "Is this because of those the papers I found locked in his desk?"

"Yes and no. They served to strengthen an ongoing investigation."

There was a pause, and Irene could hear a change in her attorney's breathing.

"The good news. He signed the divorce."

"Finally. At long last."

"Now for the bad news. His assets are frozen. Don't expect any financial support from Ashford."

CHAPTER SIXTY-FOUR

Irene pulled on her light sweat suit and sneakers, and not stopping for makeup, or even a touch of lipstick, grabbed her tote and dashed from the hotel. Rushing down the street, her only thought was of the cash in her safety deposit box. Her mind raced with possible arguments. Crossing against the traffic lights, a delivery truck swerved to avoid hitting her, a taxi screeched to a stop, and the driver leaned from the window, shouting obscenities.

Once inside the marble-floored lobby, Irene reached into the hidden zipper of her tote and withdrew her necessary key. A bank teller led her through the security gate and into the vault of stainless steel boxes, where two keys opened the door to Irene's small box. In the private room, Irene placed the long narrow box on the table and sat back. She rubbed her fingers, especially the twitching thumb.

Carefully, she lifted the lid, and stared at the neat piles of cash. Conflicting thoughts raced through her head. Here was enough cash to see her through the next three months while she looked for a real job. Hands shaking, she reached to the piles stacked one after another, but drew back, not touching the bills as though they were hot coals. Would the guilt of these wrongly obtained funds destroy her moral convictions? All her life, she'd been an ethical and honest person. Who had she become?

Irene rubbed and wrung her hands. Again, she drew a deep breath. She hadn't done anything wrong, hadn't stolen this money. But in the back of her brain, it was as though a little gnat buzzed. Deceptive by secreting the money all those years, that money had branded her as deeply as if it were an A on her chest. This money did not belong to her.

Hot and cold at the same time, her scalp was moist with perspiration. Irene barely noticed time passing. Was this her pay for all the years of wifely duties she'd endured? To rid herself of the money and its taint of deception, she'd donate the money to a charity. It would be anonymous.

Finally, her fingers trembling, she counted the neat piles of money. Should she give it all to a charity, and rid herself of the dilemma. Would that set her free of Ashford's scam? Placing her hands on the edge of the table, she closed her eyes and rocked forward and back, not reaching a decision. Would keeping half of the cash and donating the other portion solve the moral and ethical issue?

In this little space, it was hard to breathe normally. The ceiling lowered, and the walls closed in on Irene. Back into the box she placed the money, and closed the lid. She delivered it to vault and watched the bank clerk secure it with the two keys.

CHAPTER SIXTY-FIVE

Kevin, on the guitar, set a beat and rhythm for the trio while also playing an underlying melody. Julia augmented the piece with an airy theme, and Irene at the piano played with rhythmic experimentation. Their sound melded at first, but the blending developed starts and stops as Irene's mind buzzed with cross currents of uncertainty. Her fingers chased chord changes, contradicting the other instruments as if in a conversation.

Irene closed her eyes, her fingers moving across the keyboard without her giving any thought to the music or the tempo or the sound. She simply let it all go, one phrase hurtling after another, jam-packed with rumbles and crashes followed by soft touches.

At the end of their rehearsal the trio came together in an unlikely manner. Irene was running the keys with the backs of her fingers, a roller-coaster of sound challenging Julia's ending of a high note of the flute, a gorgeous sweet tone.

And then there was a stunned silence.

Kevin's eyebrows knit together. "Irene, what was that all about?"

"Just came over me."

Julia wiped the flute and looked at it as though it was foreign. "I didn't expect that at the ending."

Irene rolled her head and rubbed her fingers. "It was like you were playing a platinum flute."

Kevin fingered the scar. "It certainly was different."

Irene's hair came loose from its clip as she swivelled around on the piano bench to face Kevin. "That first melody, Kevin, sounded reminiscent of something classical, and your fingering on the strings, where did all that come from?"

"I have no idea. But I guess all the years of practice under my mother's critical eye had value. She insisted I play the violin, hated the guitar. Thought I'd join some kind of a rock group and forget all the classical training." He laughed, moving toward the kitchen. "All that training was worth it, wouldn't you say?"

Irene stood by the side of the piano. "I wouldn't know. I didn't even have a piano until I was with my uncle, and then it was an old upright. No one made me practice. Music just seemed to be in my bones. Maybe there was a musician in the family tree, but I doubt it." A little sarcastic laugh emerged. "I couldn't even read music until I was in high school, and then a teacher took me under her wing. I just caught on, it seemed easy for me."

Julia put her flute in the case and flopped down on the couch. From the kitchen, Kevin brought a silver tray and set it on the coffee table. Julia's eyes opened wide at the sight of the crystal dish of caviar set on ice, surrounded by smaller bowls of chopped egg, lemon wedges, red onion, chives, crème fraiche, and toast points.

Closing the lid on the keyboard, Irene looked at the black beads of sturgeon roe and the tiny mother of pearl spoons. Her stomach rumbled. She winced at the luxurious display. Ashford had demanded much the same exhibition of lavish wealth when he entertained associates at home. She'd often thought of the wasted money for such wanton spending. She thought only of the hungry children who lined up at the soup kitchen, their eyes devouring the mashed potatoes and gravy, sliced turkey and peas. She pulled at her twitching thumb. She should have done more than merely volunteer on the holiday.

Kevin poured three glasses of chilled champagne, handing first one to Irene and then one to Julia. He raised his own glass. "A toast. We may be the most unusual jazz trio in Manhattan."

Julia licked her lips and took a second sip of the champagne. "Yum." She leaned in toward Kevin. "This is really delicious, though I rarely have fine bubbles offered to me."

"You deserve the very best."

Though Irene took a sip, she could barely taste the sparkling champagne. Her attention strayed from the surroundings, tuning out the conversation between Julia and Kevin, and fixed on her students living in the projects, wondering what their snack would be. Probably chips. A shake of her head, she almost said aloud, "they need nutrition." She could help them.

Her forehead wrinkled as reality bombarded her runaway thoughts. She had to help herself. Survival was what she should be thinking about. Her lips drew a straight line: she was going backwards in her life. What she needed was a fresh start, a real full-time, paying job, then she could give the cash to a charity.

Irene stepped away from the piano and looked at Julia and Kevin, both oblivious to Irene's quandary. If she asked Julia, the answer would be to keep all the cash. Kevin would say to split it. Her mind went further back, knowing that in her father's greed he would have taken it without a second thought, her mother noncommittal, but her uncle might have claimed some of it earned from Ashford's legal practice. Through the mist and clouds that occupied her mind, she could see her path. Her lips turned up at the corners. Aware of her own strong heartbeat, her body felt flooded with warmth.

Irene put her glass down on the table and picked up her tote. "Sorry, guys, but I have to leave. You two, enjoy."

Julia's spoon was midway between the caviar and her mouth. "You're leaving?"

Kevin stood, his hand raised, his voice disbelieving. "I'd thought you'd stay."

Irene slung the straps onto her shoulder, and leaned in toward Kevin. "I'm sorry. There's something I have to do."

Kevin's eyebrows drew together. "Right now?"

"Right now."

CHAPTER SIXTY-SIX

Huddled in the private room at the bank, Irene carefully removed all the tied bundles of cash from her safety deposit box and placed them in ten separate plain white envelopes. Her fingertips grazed the surface of the table until at last she closed the empty metal box, stuffed the parcels into her tote, and slung the leather straps over her shoulder. From her pocket, she pulled a map of Manhattan, and reviewed the route she had sketched. Ten stops were circled in red.

The tote pressed to her side, Irene left the secure space of the bank and proceeded toward the Lower East Side. Passing narrow alleys and old dilapidated buildings, as well as chic boutiques and tenements, she noted old world fabric shops and barrels of pickles set on the cracked sidewalk, their scent bringing a tickle to her nose. Walking between parked cars, she pressed the tote with both arms tight against her chest until at last reaching her first stop, the Rescue Mission, a soup kitchen providing help for the hungry.

The air inside was filled with longing. Men, women, and children of all sizes and shapes and colors were a sea of hunger. Off to the side, standing behind a long table, were the volunteers, aprons tied around their waists, ladles lifted as they scooped steaming mounds of potatoes and chicken onto the waiting plates.

Irene was introduced to the man in charge. He was robust, with a shiny bald head and enormous smile that stretched his cheeks wide. He shook her hand, and when Irene handed the first of ten envelopes to him, he did not even glance inside the envelope to see the amount. He thanked her for the donation, saying, "Every little bit helps feed the hungry and provide hope to the homeless. We thank you."

She fingered the remaining envelopes in her tote with the sudden desire to give all the cash to this one place. Taking her hand slowly from inside the tote, she simply said, "I'm glad to have been of help."

Criss-crossing Manhattan, Irene went where meals were prepared by armies of volunteers. At each soup kitchen, she stayed just long enough to deliver the much-needed funds, graciously accepting their gratitude, humbled by the commitment of these volunteers.

Each time, Irene was blessed and hugged for her donation. Heat flooded her face with shame, remembering her previous feelings of superiority when on Christmas mornings, dressed in her finery, she would drive a few miles and serve the hungry at the local soup kitchen on Long Island, and then meet Ashford and his mother at the country club and sit amongst the plentitude of wealth. She shuddered at the recollection of having been so self-righteous for doing so little amongst so much. Her uncle once said, "A rich person should not feel superior for giving, and a poor person shouldn't feel inferior for accepting."

Nodding at the memory, Irene fondled the remaining envelope, and took a taxi to the far westside. Dropped off at a corner, she paid the driver, strode past the black iron fence, and went through the gates of the church. At the door, an attendant handed her a ticket, and welcomed her to the Soup and Soul Kitchen.

Upon entering, Irene caught a trace of stone and old wood, and years of candle wax, mixed with the scent of frankincense. Once in the sanctuary, she cast her eyes to the arching vaulted ceiling then to the tables filled mostly with men, their heads bent over plates of food. She heard the murmur of voices, low tones as though in reverence to the surroundings. A piano stood at the front of the church. It stood apart, gleaming. Colors from the stained-glass windows shone red and orange and yellow on the ebony clad grand piano. The black and white keys smiled, beckoning her.

Irene handed the last envelope to the director in charge, accepted his thanks, commented on the magnificence of the pipe organ, and asked, "The piano? Does anyone play it?"

"Of course."

"May I?"

The pastor smiled and dipped his head. "Almost every day, someone will get up and perform. Professionals and amateurs come here and play alongside someone who's just lost their home. We've had actors and musicians from the Broadway stage come and join with those less fortunate. They form a special bond, lending structure and order to the day. Everyone knows someone who's musically inclined."

He led Irene forward toward the piano. "A love of music doesn't discriminate between people. You will find playing here spiritually rewarding."

Seated on the piano bench, Irene felt her taut muscles release. She raised her hands and lightly placed them on the ivory keys. She began by playing a Debussy piece. The room quieted. The murmur of voices ceased. With her eyes half closed, she envisioned waterfalls and water lilies, the colors of a Claude Monet painting. As she played, she was deeply moved by the concentration of those seated around the tables, their silence akin to meditation.

Sharing the beauty of music, her hands danced over the keyboard, and she experienced a moment of breathtaking elation. Her heart expanded to absorb the very stillness in the sanctuary. In that surreal moment, Irene knew that in helping others, she had made the right decision.

CHAPTER SIXTY-SEVEN

Later that same evening, Irene sat with Kevin in his apartment, sipping an after-dinner brandy. Yellow tulips stood tall in a crystal vase and in the background a recording of the opera *Tosca* was playing.

Irene licked the taste of cognac on her lips. "I'm obsessed with that opera."

"Do you realize that most famous operas have a theme of unrequited love?"

She shuddered with thoughts of intrigue, secrets, and the tragic ending of *Aida*. "The romance never gets to last. Aida jumps into the deep grave to be with her lover."

"They both die, but together."

"If you think about it, none of the main characters make it out alive. Snuffed out by politics and war."

"Mostly lies and mistrust."

His words, "lies and mistrust," reverberated in her mind. She turned the snifter around and around in her moist hand, her eyes focused on the deep whirlpool of amber liquid. Truth was key in a love-filled relationship. She wanted this relationship with Kevin to be loving and lasting.

Her voice wobbled while the aria played softly, the only sound in an otherwise quiet evening.

"I have an interview tomorrow."

"That's great."

"It's secretarial, a front desk kinda thing."

"That's wasted talent."

"I need a job."

"Any company would be glad to have you, but with your talent, you should be teaching, playing professionally. If I were you, I'd hold out. That's what I would do, and nothing but. I wouldn't flit my time away like that."

She sat up and looked straight at Kevin. "You wouldn't, huh?"

"No." A chuckle rose from his chest.

"You have no idea what it's like not to have a dime or know where the next meal is coming from. I've helped at soup kitchens. You should see these people. Their eyes are empty. I always felt peaceful being able to help them, at least with nourishment." She shook her head knowing that in the past she had felt self-righteous and superior, even when giving a dollar to a beggar, or dropping a bill into the empty hat of a musician standing on the corner while the wind ripped at his tattered coat.

Kevin cleared his throat. "I acknowledge there is a good deal of poverty in this country."

"It's unacceptable while we sit here after a gourmet dinner and sip expensive cognac." Irene drew back. She hadn't meant to criticize or discredit him for his taste in expensive things. This was the way he was raised, his way of life. He didn't know any other way. "Kevin, you take everything for granted. Poverty is something you know nothing about." Softening her attitude, she smiled. "and that, dear Kevin, may be your only fault."

"No one is perfect." He kissed her forehead and pulled her back into his arms. "And that excludes you. You're perfect."

"Hardly perfect. I have plenty of faults."

"You're being very mysterious."

Irene ran the tip of her tongue over the edge of the glass, thinking of her flaws. Swirling the remaining brandy around in the snifter, she took a last sip, placed the glass on the coffee table, and turned to face Kevin.

There was a lump of fear lodged in her throat. Would her perfect image collapse with this truth? She needed to tell him. All of it. Everything. The heavy stone pressed on her chest, but she knew she had to tell him now. She wanted him to know everything about her.

"I'm far from perfect. I always thought I was a good person. But I have to tell you what a deceptive person I truly am. At least, was." She took a deep breath and dove right in. "Every week of my marriage to Ashford, I was dishonest. For fourteen years, I hid extra money, and accumulated a bundle of cash from the household budget. I hid it all for myself in a bank vault."

"You're undoubtedly not the only unhappy wife to put money away for a rainy day."

"I guess, but it gets worse. I just learned the money was stolen from his clients, their trusts and wills, money from their estates. All of that cash belonged to them. Not Ashford. Not me. Other people who had put their faith in their lawyer. And now, the IRS and the Feds are questioning him."

"He's been caught with his pants down."

"But don't you see, that's not the point. Having that money, I was a party to his unmitigated fraud."

"None of that should affect you."

Clasping her hands on her lap, her eyes sought Kevin's. "I couldn't keep or ever use that cash. I was riddled with guilt. I had to get rid of the money. So today, I went from one soup kitchen to another giving anonymous donations to each."

Kevin touched her forehead, then settled his hand on the back of her neck with a warmth of tenderness. "Why didn't you discuss all this with me?"

"I didn't want to risk you turning away from me."

"Perhaps I could have helped."

She felt the weight of his arm fall around her shoulder. Irene closed her eyes tight. "It's not in my nature to be dishonest."

"And it's not in my nature to be judgmental. Please, Irene, you should share both the good and bad with me."

Irene raised her shoulders, then shivered in a sudden sense of being unburdened. With the truth exposed, a slow smile came over her face. "I gave away every last dime of that cash to those in need. And at the last soup kitchen, you won't believe this, it's in a church on the west side. There was this piano all light with rays of sun pouring in from the stained-glass windows. It simply called to me. I could hear it saying, "Play me. Play me. Play me." And I went past the tables of men and women bent over their plates of food, and I played that piano while they sat quietly finishing their meal. It was glorious."

Not certain she wanted to disclose anything further, Irene shifted on the couch. "I know it sounds tacky, but it felt as though I'd just taken a long, hot shower and was cleansed."

The smile overcame Irene's face. Her heart pumping, delight danced in her eyes. "You should have heard it. I wish you'd been there. Next time you'll come with me. The tone of that piano was so rich. It filled the sanctuary with joy and hope, as if the music was my voice, giving them a few moments of happiness and courage. It felt awesome."

"Sounds like you had a good day." Kevin cocked his head, smiled, and wrapped both his arms around Irene. He murmured in her ear, "I only care that you are here with me now and we're together, faults or not. We all have baggage from our past. What's done is done."

He kissed her forehead, her eyelids, her long neck just below her ear, and whispered, "We shouldn't let anything interfere with our happiness. As long as we're together…"

All the tension and stress left her body. Freed of the last vestige of guilt, she curled into Kevin's embrace, kissing his mouth with a tenderness that grew as he slipped his hand down her back and pressed her to him, the kiss slowly igniting their passion. Irene knew they were meant to be one, share their life with one another, and that nothing would ever stand between them or pull them apart. They were inseparable.

He drew back, and held her face lovingly between his palms. "Don't take that nonsensical job."

"Why? I need a job." She smiled and waited.

"Move in here with me."

Irene drew back, unable to answer.

"I mean it. Move out of that God-awful hotel, and come be with me here."

"Oh, Kevin, I can't do that."

"I want to share my life with you. I'll take care of you."

She placed a palm on his shoulder. "I don't want you to take care of me." She must make him understand that she must first learn to take care of herself.

"You're turning me down?"

"Kevin, you're a wonderful man, and I do want to be with you. But I can't move in here." She shook her head, and watched as he glanced from her to the carpet to the ceiling and then fingered the little scar on his forehead. She watched the smile fade from his face, the wrinkles around his eyes deepen. She could feel a barrier was building between them. She didn't want this to happen.

"Kevin, I do love you, please know that. To be with you fills my heart. But don't you see, I have to find my own way, be strong before I can truly be yours. I've only just begun rebuilding myself."

She placed both of her palms on his chest, and felt his body shift further away, stiffen under her touch. Fear tightened in her stomach and chest. "I've only just begun to think for myself, own myself. Until I feel secure in and of myself, I must be on my own. Please don't turn away from me." She pressed her cheek against his chest, and felt his rapid heartbeat. She wrapped her arms tight around his waist.

Irene felt his chest rise up and down. She held on with all the inner strength she could muster, and did not let go until she felt the muscles, the very core of Kevin's body, begin to relax. She waited with longing as Kevin took long, slow breaths, filling his lungs with their future.

Dancer to Writer—Choreographer to Author

Ms. Shulman began her career fully engaged in the world of dance as a choreographer and performer with various professional companies. After retiring from the stage, her attention turned to the written word and she began writing in earnest. Numerous short stories have been published in various magazines and newspapers. Themes of family, love, and desire are evident in her published novels.

Other Books by Bunny Shulman

Timed Exposures
On My Eyes
Turning Point
Step By Step
Muse On Madison
Keira's Story

CPSIA information can be obtained
at www.ICGtesting.com
Printed in the USA
BVHW071002150419
545534BV00004B/587/P

9 781515 423867